About the

Alan Gorevan is an award-winning writer and intellectual property attorney. He lives in Dublin. Visit his website at www.alangorevan.com

By Alan Gorevan

NOVELS:
Out of Nowhere
Better Confess

NOVELLAS:
The Forbidden Room
The Hostage
Hit and Run

SHORT STORY COLLECTION:
Dark Tales

Better Confess

Alan Gorevan

BETTER CONFESS

CHAPTER ONE

Dublin. Thursday, 6:54 pm.
Florence Lynch took a bottle of perfume from her handbag and gave her neck a discreet squirt of Chanel No. 5. The fragrance had been her late mother's favourite, and Florence liked to keep a bottle of it with her at all times.

The taxi driver glanced at her in his mirror.

"Going somewhere nice?"

He was a leathery-faced man in his fifties, with tufty, greying hair. Florence ignored him. A stranger had no business knowing her plans. She placed a breath mint on the tip of her tongue and gazed at the driver's face in the mirror.

They thought they had a right to ask anything they liked. As bad as hairdressers, Florence thought, though at least her hairdresser stuck to asking if Florence had any holiday plans and what she was doing at the weekend.

"Excuse me," she said, pulling out her iPhone. She brought the screen to life, lighting up the gloomy backseat of the taxi.

"Sure, sure," the driver said.

He yawned obnoxiously. Even if she hadn't been a coach to small-business owners, Florence would have been appalled by his lack of professionalism. People never seemed to think about the impression they made.

Florence always made sure to present herself optimally when she met clients: looking well-groomed, smelling pleasant, smiling and alert, after a solid night's sleep. She drank two litres of water each day to keep her teenage acne in the past tense, and had her hair styled at an exclusive salon every two weeks. As far as appearances went, she had little to worry about, though some days the gap between her front teeth preoccupied her. She had a tall, athletic build, an upright carriage and long, honey-coloured hair.

At thirty, Florence knew she was on the brink of personal and professional triumph. Her bachelor's degree in communications and her master's in marketing had set her on a trajectory towards success. Always striving for improvement, she liked to share what she'd learned with others.

"You shouldn't yawn like that," Florence said, unable to resist. "It's incredibly rude."

"Pardon?" the driver said. From his tone of voice, Florence gathered that he had heard her, but was too stung to believe he'd heard her correctly.

Florence's iPhone rang.

"Never mind," she said. "I have to take this."

"Sure, sure."

She noted the time displayed on her phone, then put it to her ear. "What is it, Jill?"

Jill Fitzgibbon, Florence's personal assistant, stayed in the office until at least nine o'clock every night, though no one asked her to do this. Florence couldn't say she liked Jill. The younger woman was too nervous, calling Florence constantly, even out of hours. However, Florence's father had appointed her, and he hated it when Florence questioned his hiring and firing decisions.

"Sorry to bother you," Jill said.

Despite her shyness, Jill always spoke loudly, as if to compensate.

"What is it?"

"I was about to leave the office when I got an urgent e-mail from Jon Glynn."

Florence groaned. Jon Glynn, a new client, liked to have his hand held. Florence had spent far too much of her morning in a meeting with him, listening to his plans for his IT company. Florence found the inner workings of computers tedious, not to mention baffling.

"What does he want?"

"He says he needs to speak to you at once."

"Well, I'll talk to him tomorrow."

"His e-mail does say *at once*. I just thought you should know."

"Does he say why?"

"He's worried about his trade mark. He says it's been rejected by the Intellectual Property Office."

"Big deal," Florence said.

"What should I tell him?"

"Don't tell him anything. Let him wait until tomorrow."

"Okay," Jill said with a nervous laugh. She drew the word out, as if she was giving herself time to think of an argument.

Florence ended the call.

"Trouble at home?" the driver asked.

Florence glared at the back of his head, at the point where grey tufts receded into pink skin.

As if he had any right to know whether Florence had trouble at home, or anywhere else for that matter.

She gazed out the window. The taxi was moving slowly through Dublin's north inner city. They were now on Capel Street, approaching Simon's office.

"I said, trouble at home?" the driver repeated, as if she owed him an answer.

"Never mind that. Can you go any faster?"

The driver shrugged. "Only if the car in front does."

Florence fished around in her handbag for her lipstick, and applied a little more.

The truth was that things were wonderful at home. Florence had no reason to complain. Simon Hill was the perfect boyfriend. Sometimes he could be silly – just look at his ridiculous man-bun and his obsession with milkshakes – but he had a good heart.

Tonight, Florence was treating Simon to dinner at a new ramen bar she'd wanted to try for months. Simon had already been there at lunchtime and he insisted the place served the best noodles in the city.

The taxi passed Simon's workplace, the headquarters of marketing company, Transcend Promotions. It was an old building. Though not much to look at, Florence felt happy every time she saw the place. Not only did her boyfriend work there, but so did her best friend, Hazel Price. Hazel was the one who introduced Simon to Florence.

The taxi began to move a little faster.

"Do you have any plans for the weekend?" the driver asked.

Florence sighed.

"Could you—"

Could you shut your mouth? she thought.

But then she was distracted. Out the window, she saw a man who looked like Simon walking along the sun-dappled footpath.

No, it *was* Simon, and he was arm-in-arm with a woman in a short black skirt. The woman turned her head and Florence saw that it was Hazel.

Perhaps they had left work together.

Florence stared at her boyfriend and her best friend. Why were they so close to each other? Their arms were linked and they were laughing hard.

And, as Florence watched, Hazel threw her arms around Simon and kissed him on the lips.

CHAPTER TWO

London. Thursday, 6:55 pm.

"Sir, when a man is tired of London," Samuel Johnson wrote, "he is tired of life; for there is in London all that life can afford."

Thomas Ogden had always thought that was true. London throbbed with energy, with variety, with vitality. And right now, Thomas was in the perfect place to observe the great city's masses. He'd managed to snag the window seat in a trendy new coffee shop near Trafalgar Square. His chair was angled towards the window and his laptop rested on his knees. An endless flood of people hurried past the window, umbrellas raised against the evening's misty rain.

With his hoodie and jeans, his short brown hair, upturned nose and thick-rimmed glasses, Thomas Ogden looked exactly like a computer programmer, but this was his uniform. His mask. Though he was in fact an IT professional, it wasn't natural for him to dress like one.

Oddly enough, he preferred to clothe himself in a well-cut suit rather than a T-shirt or chinos. It was a relic of having a tailor for a father. Thomas only dressed casually when he didn't want to be seen.

The light next to Thomas's chair was angled away so his face would not be lit up, either to passers-by on the street or to the other customers in the café. Thomas's work was important, and it demanded invisibility.

He took a sip of coffee. It had turned cold while he sat there. Wincing, he dribbled the bitter beverage back into the mug. He glanced around. The café was busy, but no one was paying any attention to him. Trying to get rid of the taste in his mouth, he dribbled the last bitter dregs back into the cup, then set it down on the table in front of him.

He glanced at the restaurant across the road. It was a French place specialising in *small plates*, whatever that meant. Thomas had been watching the yellow glow of its window for an hour.

The target's name was Brook Reynolds. He sat at the third table from the window, against the left wall. A Toulouse-Lautrec print hung on the wall over his head.

Normally on Thursday evenings, Mr. Reynolds visited his mistress's Vauxhall apartment on the way home from work. His wife thought he played badminton. She was usually busy marking assignments, though her browser history showed an unhealthy fixation on cat videos.

Thomas knew all about the couple.

When it came to his work, Thomas lived by certain simple rules, about which he was completely inflexible.

He had to make sure he had the right target. The target was guaranteed dead within twenty-four hours. No cancellations. No refunds.

Normally Thomas had little time to observe the target. He had to do the best he could within the limit, using both physical and technological surveillance. Usually that yielded sufficient information.

In this case, the client had approached them with a query, and then a number of weeks passed before the booking was made.

During that time, Thomas's curiosity had remained piqued. He had no other target during this period, and was becoming restless, so he took it upon himself to do some preliminary research.

Mr. Reynolds and his wife turned out to be a well-off couple in their fifties. They lived in a plush townhouse in West Brompton and had no children. Reynolds's wife was a popular biochemistry lecturer at a nearby university. Mr. Reynolds was a portfolio manager who looked after endowments for a (different) university.

Thomas wondered if Mr. Reynolds had met his wife through work. It was certainly how he met his mistress.

On Saturdays, Mr. Reynolds played golf. On Sundays, he sang in a church choir, then met his mistress again under the pretext of visiting an elderly relative, whose care facility was conveniently nearby.

Thomas had gleaned excellent information about the man's movements from the location history on his phone.

Mr. Reynolds's e-mails and text messages showed that he was sick of his wife but feared a messy, expensive divorce.

It was all so drearily predictable, Thomas reflected.

He observed beads of rain running down the windowpane. The dark clouds made the summer evening gloomier than it would otherwise have been.

Today, Mr. Reynolds and three friends were having dinner. Or *small plates*, whatever that meant. The French restaurant had about two dozen tables, all of which were occupied. Lots of witnesses. Thomas had been tempted to get a table in the restaurant himself, but decided it was too risky, so had settled on the café opposite. He had to be careful. He took elaborate precautions for the online side of this business. It would be crazy not to exercise proper caution for the physical part of the plan too.

Thomas checked the time.

Eighteen hours had passed since the booking came through. He'd received his cut of the fee in bitcoin before the job. They always charged half in advance, with the understanding that the remaining half would be transferred as soon as the target was dead. Thomas kept half of the initial payment and the organisation kept the other half. Thomas wasn't sure that was a fair split, but he wasn't greedy.

Thomas hadn't been able to sleep because of the excitement. Even after all the jobs he had done, each new one was a thrill.

"Don't cause any more pain than you have to," the client had said. Thomas took professional pride in fulfilling clients' instructions.

Across the street, Mr. Reynolds and his friends were finishing their meal. It hadn't taken long. Now Thomas knew what *small plates* meant. It meant a small meal and a big bill. He watched as the waiter brought them a fresh set of menus.

Time for coffee, Thomas thought. *And I'll supply dessert: a nice, painless murder.*

CHAPTER THREE

Dublin. Thursday, 7:15 pm.
Florence Lynch stared out the window of the taxi. She couldn't believe what she was seeing. Simon and Hazel, their lips locked together, then pulling back, gazing into each other's eyes. They looked so happy. For a moment, Florence could do nothing but stare in horror.

They're having an affair.

As Florence watched, Simon threw his arms around Hazel and they hugged. She couldn't help thinking what a handsome couple they made. Her best friend and her boyfriend.

Simon stood six feet tall and carried himself in a way that was self-assured without ever becoming arrogant. He had an easy-going charm and his long, black hair framed a sweet smile that let him get away with anything.

Hazel, on the other hand, was good-looking in a less obvious way. She had round cheeks, a button nose, and shoulder-length chestnut-brown hair that framed a triangular face. If she didn't have a great sense of style, Hazel made up for it with her vitality. She was constantly trying exciting new things: skydiving, skiing, ziplining, paintballing, go-cart racing. Guys loved that about her. It had always been a mystery to Florence why Hazel hadn't settled down with one of her boyfriends yet.

Now Florence knew the reason. Hazel wanted to steal Simon away from her. Or she already had.

Is it serious? How long has it been going on?

Florence had a thousand questions.

She'd been dating Simon for two years. They'd been talking about buying a house together. Had he been cheating on her the whole time, or was this a recent development?

How could he *do* this to her?

The taxi began to move faster.

"Hey, wait!" Florence snapped. They'd been crawling along for half an hour, and the idiot behind the wheel chose this exact moment to start speeding? "Stop the car."

The driver turned his head slowly, and said, "What?"

They'd left Simon and Hazel behind.

Florence leaned forward in her seat.

"Stop the car immediately. I want to get out."

"I can't stop here." The driver glanced at her in the mirror. Florence couldn't help thinking that there was a hint of amusement on his face, as if he enjoyed seeing her get flustered. "There are cars behind us," he added.

"Just let me jump out."

"Give me a minute and I'll find somewhere to pull over."

Florence stopped herself from slapping him on the side of the head, as she felt sorely tempted to do. Her life was on the line, and he acted like everything was alright.

She turned and peered through the back windscreen, but Simon and Hazel were no longer in sight. The car was moving too quickly, and Florence realised they had nearly reached the ramen bar.

Fine, she would go there, where she was supposed to meet Simon anyway. She could ask Simon where he'd been, what he had been doing, and see what he had to say for himself.

"Never mind," Florence said. "Continue on."

"Sure, sure."

They reached the place after another couple of minutes. Florence jumped out of the car as soon as it stopped. Though it was a warm June evening, she closed her coat across her chest and glanced around.

The street was full of small shops and restaurants. From the outside, the ramen bar looked clean and modern, with a black paint job and a neon sign over the doorway.

"Hello?" a man shouted.

Florence turned to find the taxi driver getting out of his car.

"What do you want?" she asked.

"I'm not a charity."

"What?"

"You didn't pay me."

The man didn't look sleepy now. His face was pink and angry. He was a big guy and his belly hung over the belt of his trousers. His bulk and attitude made her nervous.

Florence said, "I have other things on my mind."

"Sure, sure. You're busy dolling yourself up."

"Excuse me," she snapped. "I don't like your tone."

She found the cash in her purse and handed it to him. He grabbed it out of her hand, and got back behind the wheel, grumbling as he went. She had expected some small amount of change, not to mention a thank you, but the man drove off at once.

"Outrageous service," Florence muttered.

Two young men in tracksuits stood a little way up the street, smoking. One of them noticed Florence and whistled at her.

She decided to wait inside the restaurant. After all, she needed a moment to compose herself. She didn't want Simon to think she was upset.

The men walked over to her.

"Hey, sexy woman," the whistler said. "Want a smoke?"

"No, I don't want a smoke," Florence replied. "Leave me alone."

The man who had spoken laughed.

"She's fiery," he told his friend.

"Yeah, she is."

Florence took a step towards the restaurant, but the whistler blocked her way.

"How about a kiss?" he asked.

This is too much, Florence decided.

She grabbed the man's hoodie and jabbed the corner of her iPhone up his nostril. He tilted his head back in surprise, but Florence held onto him and pushed the phone harder.

"I told you to leave me alone."

She released him and gave a push with the phone. The man stumbled back onto the ground.

Florence's phone was wet with snot. She looked at it in disgust, then at the two men, who broke out laughing. That just made her angrier.

Temper, temper.

Her friends knew that when she was mad, Florence could do anything. Holding her phone down by her side, she entered the restaurant.

CHAPTER FOUR

London. Thursday, 7:26 pm.

Thomas Ogden watched Brook Reynolds step out of the French restaurant. He and his dining partners stood on the footpath for a minute saying their goodbyes. They were all middle-aged men who had the look of success about them.

Reynolds was the most conspicuously handsome. He wore a navy suit with a white shirt. Pointy black shoes that shone like mirrors. His back was ramrod straight, and even from a distance, he looked like a man who commanded respect.

Reynolds stood in the way of passing pedestrians, forcing them to go around him on the crowded footpath. He seemed oblivious, standing with his shoulders thrust back and wide smile on his face, paying no attention whatsoever to the passers-by.

The man's misplaced sense of entitlement only confirmed the opinion Thomas had already formed.

Brook Reynolds deserved to die – not someday, not of old age – but tonight, at Thomas Ogden's hand.

Reynolds and his friends broke up and went their separate ways.

Thomas slipped his laptop in its bag and slung it over his shoulder before hurrying out of the café. Misty rain was still falling. The air was full of the honking of car horns.

Thomas walked to the pedestrian lights and crossed the road. It was easy to blend into the crowd. He didn't look like an assassin, and he was sure that no one thought he was following Reynolds. But it always paid to be cautious.

Keeping well back, Thomas followed Reynolds as he headed west, walking at a leisurely pace. He knew exactly why Reynolds was in no hurry to get home, and it made him sick with rage.

At Embankment, he followed Reynolds down the steps to the Underground station. Thomas scanned his Oyster card and passed through the turnstiles and down to the platform, where Reynolds would catch a District Line train.

The distinctive, musty smell of the Tube station filled Thomas's nostrils. As always, it was stiflingly hot down there.

Reynolds took out his phone and put in his ear buds.

A train shot out of the tunnel in the usual terrifying manner, headlights blazing, its sound huge in the enclosed space.

Thomas stepped back.

Perhaps strangely for a hired killer, Thomas was terrified of dying down here. He was always afraid of falling on the tracks and being crushed by an oncoming train, afraid that someone might push him. He was damned if he was going to let that happen.

When the doors opened, he stepped onto the train and watched as Reynolds found a seat at the far end of the carriage.

Thomas zeroed in on one too. He sat down and took out his phone. It wasn't necessary to watch Reynolds too closely, as he knew that the portfolio manager wouldn't be going anywhere for a while.

Thomas opened up the Better Confess website. Business had been slow, so lately Thomas had gone looking for it, instead of letting it come to him. Better Confess had become his favourite hunting ground. It had already yielded a couple of jobs.

He liked the website's simplicity. There was nothing to it, really. An anonymous forum where people confessed to things they had done or wanted to do. If Thomas saw something juicy, he left a comment under the post, offering to help. Once in a while, when venting wasn't enough, someone replied. Then things got interesting.

As the train shot down the dark tunnel, Thomas browsed the latest confessions. They could be sorted by category or by which ones were most recent. Sadly, most of the posts were mundane. He scanned through them quickly.

My 2-year old is driving me crazy. Sometimes I wish I never had him. Does that make me a bad mother?

The train passed Westminster, then Victoria Station. Thomas kept reading.

I had a fling with my tennis coach. I feel so guilty. I want to tell my husband but I don't know if he'll forgive me.

These whiners reminded Thomas of the political crowd he'd hung around with at university. Despite his computer science degree, it was the arts students he'd drank with in the pub. For a while he'd felt like one of them. He used to carry around a copy of *The Communist Manifesto* and spout off about the exploitation of the proles, even though he and his family enjoyed a comfortable life and no one actually seemed to be exploiting him. It embarrassed him to think of it now.

In January, there had been an interesting post on Better Confess. A salesman left a furious rant about an office rival. Thomas replied with an offer to help and the man took him up on it. The man had no problem with any rival now.

Thomas kept reading. Nothing caught his attention, but the journey passed quickly all the same.

Soon the train came to a stop at West Brompton, an above-ground station. Weak as it was, the June light momentarily blinded Thomas as it streamed in the windows of the carriage.

He took his time walking to the door, letting Brook Reynolds disembark before him. Commuters jostled Thomas when he finally got off. He pushed through the mass of people and caught a glimpse of Brook Reynolds walking briskly out onto the street. Thomas felt a frisson of alarm.

Was Reynolds hurrying?

Did he know he was being followed?

Thomas increased his own speed. He jogged to the turnstile and scanned his Oyster card. The machine rejected it with an unhappy beep. Thomas scanned the card again but it failed. He broke out in a sweat. He had to get out of here. He moved to a different machine. Thankfully, this one accepted his card.

He hurried out to the street. There were plenty of people around but no sign of the target. Thomas knew exactly where Reynolds lived. He had parked his van near the house early that morning, anticipating a fast getaway. But he needed to ambush Reynolds before he got home or the plan was dead.

Thomas set off down the road towards Brompton Cemetery, a beautiful old garden cemetery that Reynolds liked to cut through on his way home.

There was no one about now.

Thomas walked under the stone archway leading into the cemetery and walked straight into Brook Reynolds.

CHAPTER FIVE

Dublin. Thursday, 7:27 pm.
Once inside the ramen restaurant, Florence found herself in a small reception area with an unattended till. A figurine of a cat sat on the counter, one paw raised in the air.

PLEASE WAIT TO BE SEATED, read a sign.

Florence counted the seconds while she waited for someone to appear. She stopped at 10, because that was already unacceptable. She would have walked out of the place if she wasn't waiting for Simon.

A folding screen with pink orchids painted on it divided the area from the rest of the restaurant, and a padded two-seat couch lay in front of the till. Florence walked around the side of the screen.

The main restaurant area opened out in front of her, consisting of about twenty tables, each with a flickering candle and two chairs. A window to the kitchen was inset in the wall at the end of the room. Florence saw a flash of flame on a frying pan.

The sound of sizzling food made Florence's mouth water. The wonderful smell of fried tuna steak drifted to her.

Two waitresses and a waiter stood talking near the hatch to the kitchen.

While Florence stood at the side of the room, waiting for them to greet her, she glanced around, taking in the glossy black walls adorned with sketches of Mount Fuji. Music was playing low, but it was hard to make out over the buzz of conversation.

"Excuse me?" Florence said, in the crystal tone she used at office meetings. Her voice carried all the way to the chef, who cocked an eyebrow. A few diners looked up. The waiting staff didn't seem to notice though. Florence felt they were ignoring her deliberately.

She decided to seat herself. She walked over to an empty table. It had not been cleaned since the previous diner left. There was rice and other debris scattered all over the tabletop. Florence turned away from it. She could feel the eyes of the other diners.

Why are they looking at me like that? Florence thought. *Do they think I'm going to make a scene?*

Another empty table caught her eye, this one on the other side of the room. Holding her head high, she walked over to the table. This one was clean. She took off her coat and hung it on a hook on the wall, then sat down, ignoring the RESERVED placard in the middle of the table.

Had Simon been alone when he came here, or did he come here with Hazel? Had they sat opposite each other, with a candle between them on the table?

How romantic.

A waitress appeared by Florence's side. A young Asian woman with short hair and dimples. Florence held out her hand for a menu.

The girl waved her hands, smiling nervously. She said, "I'm so sorry. This table is reserved."

"Excuse me?"

"You can't sit here. The table is reserved. You can wait in the reception area."

Florence could imagine the humiliation of vacating the table, heading back outside with everyone watching, everyone laughing at her.

"No, I certainly won't."

"It's reserved," the girl said slowly.

Florence felt her cheeks turn pink. "I understand what you're saying. *I* reserved it. I'm a customer."

"You have a booking?"

"Yes, in the name of my…" Florence swallowed. "It's in the name of Simon Hill."

The girl gave a nervous laugh. "Let me check," she said.

"Bring me a glass of Chardonnay while I'm waiting."

"Okay, let me check."

Florence changed her mind. "Actually, bring a bottle."

The table was set with two forks and two knives at each place. Florence picked up a fork. It was stainless steel, and a decent weight. She scrutinised it closely to make sure it was clean. Satisfied, she set it back down.

Next she picked up the knife. It had a serrated edge, and a sharp point. A steak knife. She stared at the blade while she waited for Simon to arrive.

CHAPTER SIX

Dublin. Thursday, 7:31 pm.
Simon was five minutes late reaching the restaurant. Picking out the ring in Bartley's had taken longer than expected. The salesman, Will, had been such good company, and so helpful, that the time had just flown by. Simon quickened his pace. Florence was a stickler for punctuality, but today Simon had an excellent excuse.

He passed two junkies on the street. The men, deep in conversation, didn't so much as look at him. He hoped Florence hadn't encountered them. Sometimes she rubbed people up the wrong way. Her temper was really…

Whatever.

Simon had something that would put a smile on her face.

His coat pocket was large enough to hold the ornate bag from Bartley's, which was a relief because even the bag was beautiful. It would have been a shame to have to ditch it. Simon could hardly wait to see Florence's face when she saw the ring. He'd been thinking about this moment for weeks. Now it was so close. He wasn't sure he could wait until after dinner to propose. Maybe he'd do it immediately.

He stepped into the restaurant. The till area was empty, but the buzz of conversation carried to him from the tables beyond. He let the door swing shut and waited for someone to come and seat him.

He was looking forward to dinner with Florence, but, more than that, he looked forward to getting down on one knee and asking her to be his wife.

He wanted her by his side for the rest of his life.

Every day.

Every hour.

He hoped she'd like the ring. Hazel had guided him, which was great because jewellery was so baffling. It was impossible to just ask for an engagement ring. Or even to ask for a gold or silver ring. There were so many precious metals these days. Simon's brain short-circuited when he saw the little labels stating *rose gold, yellow gold, round cut, radiant cut…*

Luckily, Hazel was an enthusiastic window-shopper. She seemed almost as excited about the engagement as Simon.

"I'll be waiting to hear how it goes," she'd said as they hugged and went their separate ways a few minutes earlier.

"I'm sure you'll be Florence's first call," Simon replied. "You and her father."

"You mean her daddy," Hazel said with a laugh.

Simon thought that *daddy* was a word you needed to purge from your vocabulary by the time you became an adult, but Florence insisted on using it.

"Good evening."

A young man appeared from the dining area.

"Hello. My name is Simon Hill. I have a reservation."

The man went behind the counter and tapped a screen.

"Oh yes," he said. "Your... friend is here..."

Something about the waiter's tone gave Simon pause for thought. But the waiter quickly picked out a menu and gestured for Simon to follow. Simon took a breath and patted his pocket. The ring was still there, thank goodness. He didn't want to lose the thing after spending so much money on it.

He followed the waiter into the main dining area. The atmosphere seemed just as he'd remembered from last time. Music, candles, everything.

But then Florence caught his eye, sitting at a table at the side of the room. Broken glass and spilled wine covered the tabletop.

CHAPTER SEVEN

London. Thursday, 7:31 pm.
Under the arched entrance to Brompton Cemetery, Brook Reynolds was pacing from side to side, talking on his phone, his arm extended, finger jabbing the evening air. When Thomas Ogden turned into the cemetery, they nearly collided. Reynolds's finger almost poked Thomas in the eye. He felt the displaced air on his face. Reynolds didn't even notice. He continued pacing from side to side.

"Because the dean doesn't understand currency swaps," Reynolds snapped. "Of course not. He's a sociology professor, for god's sake. I get that. Yeah, so what?"

The sign on the gate said that the cemetery closed at eight o'clock.

Tight, but possible.

Thomas walked past Reynolds. A broad path called the Central Avenue stretched into the distance, cutting a straight line through the cemetery.

Graves and leafy trees lined both sides of the Avenue. Fresh flowers had been laid at the cross marking the grave of Emmeline Pankhurst. Thomas admired them for a moment, then continued down the Avenue. Despite the misty rain, the garden cemetery looked beautiful in the dim light.

After a minute, Thomas stepped off the path, onto the wet grass. Tens of thousands of monuments to the dead surrounded him. He picked his way through the tombstones until he was about thirty feet from the path.

There he waited for Brook Reynolds.

A bell rang in the distance, warning that closing time approached. For a moment, terror seized Thomas, and he wondered if Reynolds would backtrack out of the cemetery, given that the gates would close soon.

But a moment later, Reynolds appeared, walking briskly down the path. Thomas smiled to himself. He should have known that a man like Reynolds wouldn't worry about obeying any rule that would inconvenience him. Reynolds's phone rang again, its harsh ringtone sounding obscene in this place of peace. While Reynolds answered, Thomas began to walk parallel to the path, letting Reynolds get slightly ahead.

He slipped on a pair of latex gloves.

The place was almost deserted, and Thomas began to edge closer to the path.

The tail of Reynolds's expensive suit jacket couldn't conceal his flabby backside. Despite his handsome features, he'd grown bloated from sucking the blood out of others. In time, if left to his own devices, he would leave his wife a shell of her former self. His mistress too, probably.

But Reynolds would not be left to his own devices.

Thomas stepped back onto the Avenue as they approached a giant yew tree. They were nearly at the Fulham Road end of the cemetery.

Reynolds came to a stop while he spoke intently into the phone. Thomas kept edging silently closer.

"See you tomorrow," Reynolds said. "Bye."

Thomas was right behind him.

You won't see anyone tomorrow.

Thomas pulled the pistol from his shoulder holster, took off the safety, and screwed on the silencer.

He aimed the 9mm at Reynolds's head. The older man sensed someone behind him, and turned slowly.

"Your wallet," Thomas said.

Reynolds's mouth went slack. The gun was like a black hole, sucking his eyes towards it.

"Toss your wallet on the ground," Thomas said, enunciating each word slowly. He glanced up and down the Avenue.

No one around, but he couldn't stand here all day.

Seeming to recover himself, Reynolds jabbed a finger at the gun. "I'm not going to be intimidated."

"Okay," Thomas said, and shot him.

A single neat hole appeared in Reynolds's forehead. He lurched back onto the ground like a tipped cow. Thomas hurried to his side.

Reynolds's eyes were open and he was dead.

Thomas slipped the gun back into its holster, and patted Reynolds's trouser pockets. Found the one with the wallet. He stuffed the wallet in his pocket, next to his own, and set off jogging down the Avenue, only slowing when he approached the gate. One side of it was closed. Thomas was just in time.

He slipped outside, his heart racing, and turned right, away from the petrol station that lay opposite the cemetery. Once he had gone on a little bit, he took out Reynolds' wallet and threw it in the garden of a house.

A little favour to the police, making it easy to identify the body.

He removed his gloves and walked down the road.

Job done, with hours to spare.

CHAPTER EIGHT

Dublin. Thursday, 7:55 pm.

Florence used her napkin to sweep the broken glass and spilled Chardonnay off the table. The waitress stepped back to avoid getting splashed.

"Stupid girl," Florence said. "Look what you've done."

Florence had fumbled with the bottle when she went to pour herself a glass. The waitress should have poured it instead of just slapping the bottle on the table and leaving it to wobble in front of her. This wasn't the kind of service Florence expected in any decent restaurant.

The waitress laughed.

She was actually *laughing* at Florence.

"What are you waiting for? Clean this up and get me a fresh bottle. I expect it to be on the house."

Once the waitress had hurried away, Florence noticed that the wine had got on her dress too. Well, the restaurant would have to pay for her dry cleaning.

That was a fact. Other diners were watching. A man at the next table had paused with a forkful of pork halfway to his mouth.

"What? Eat your food," she snapped. "At least you have your meal. Moron."

The man turned his attention back to his food.

"What happened?"

Florence whipped her head up as Simon and a waiter reached the table.

Even now, Florence couldn't help noticing what a dashing figure Simon cut. He wore a long black coat over a dark suit.

"Is everything okay?" Simon asked.

He took the seat opposite her.

"We'll get this cleaned up right away," the waiter said before hurrying away.

Florence glared at Simon. Perhaps there was an innocent explanation for what she had seen, though she couldn't imagine what it might be. Simon had been hugging and kissing Hazel, and there was no good reason for her boyfriend to be hugging and kissing anyone but her. She decided she'd wait for him bring it up.

"Well?" Simon prompted.

She waved her hand in the general direction of the kitchen.

"The waitress made a mess."

Simon smiled. "We can't let that ruin our evening."

He leaned across the table to kiss her. Florence imagined those lips locked on Hazel's. She shuddered and pretended not to notice what Simon was doing. Instead, she reached into her pocket for a tissue and wiped her hands. Simon leaned back in his seat again, an expression of confused disappointment on his face.

"I don't like this place," Florence said.

"Wait until you try the food. The sushi here is to die for. Did you order a whole bottle of wine?"

Florence straightened her back. "Yes."

"Oh. Okay."

"How's everything at the office?"

"Fine," Simon said.

The way he kept smiling was infuriating. It must have been because of Hazel. Did he love her so much? Did she do something for him that Florence never had?

Florence still remembered the time Hazel stole her boyfriend, back when they were in school together. She'd hated Hazel for a while. But that was all behind them, years ago. And later they'd become best friends.

Florence said, "Did you come straight here from work?"

"Yes," Simon said. "Sorry for the delay. Something kept me late."

Yeah, something kept you late. Hazel's tongue.

Florence stopped grinding her teeth for a moment, to say, "Did you leave work alone?"

"Yeah. Why?"

A waitress came and wiped the table down, sweeping the remaining broken glass into a plastic bin and cleaning off the surface of the table with a cloth. She used a dustpan and brush on the floor, then hurried away.

Another waiter appeared with a fresh bottle of wine and a replacement glass for Florence. He poured a small amount for each of them, without offering to let either of them try it. The wine could have been corked. In this place, it probably was, but that was the least of her problems.

Florence picked up the glass and drained it. The waiter hadn't time to put the bottle down.

"Fill my glass," Florence said.

She glared at Simon, amazed at his duplicity. He'd been cavorting on the street with her best friend just a moment ago and now he was lying to her so smoothly. She never would have believed he was cheating on her unless she'd seen it. When did Simon learn to lie so well?

The waiter topped up her glass, set the bottle on the table, and hurried away.

"What is it?" Simon asked. "What's wrong?"

"What are you so cheerful about?"

Simon shrugged, then tapped his coat pocket. "Nothing," he said. "Just glad to be here with you."

"Wouldn't you prefer to be with Hazel?"

"What?"

"You heard me. You lied. You said you walked here alone."

"Keep your voice down," he said, glancing to the side.

The other diners were looking at Florence again.

"I will not," Florence shouted. "Don't tell me what to do, you cheater!"

She grabbed her glass and threw the wine in his face. He gasped as it splashed his cheek and dribbled down onto his shirt.

"Florence, I came here to—"

"I don't care," she said. "You came here and lied to me."

"Why are you so upset?"

"I know you're cheating on me with Hazel!"

"What? I'm—"

"You kissed her. You hugged her. I feel sick looking at you."

She waited a moment, wondering what Simon had to say for himself. Usually when they had an argument, Simon let her cool down, and then he knew just the right words to put things right.

However, now his expression hardened.

"You don't trust me at all, do you?" Simon asked.

"Not when you lie to me. How long has it been going on?"

Simon shook his head. "Maybe this was a bad idea."

"What's a bad idea? Cheating on me? Yeah, it's a bad idea, you jerk."

"You're not mature enough—"

"Not mature enough for what?"

The waitress appeared beside them.

"Are we ready to order?" she said, her pen and notebook poised to write.

Florence stared at her in amazement. If she were training the owner of this business, her first piece of advice would be to fire the staff.

"Do we look like we're ready to order? Go away."

"Florence—" Simon began.

She jabbed her index finger at him. "Don't mess me around. Tell me the truth. How long have you and Hazel been sneaking around behind my back?"

"Oh my god," Simon muttered.

"Well?"

"Forget it," Simon said. A hard look passed over his face. He stood up and put his coat on.

"What are you doing? Where are you going?"

"Off to meet Hazel, according to you."

"Tell me the truth, then."

"Forget it." Simon waved his hands in a vague gesture. "Forget everything."

He took out his wallet, picked two bills out of it, and left them on the table. Then he turned and walked straight out of the restaurant.

CHAPTER NINE

London. Thursday, 8:01 pm.
The rain had eased and the evening was now bright. Thomas Ogden sat in his van, watching the Reynolds house. The van was parked next to a beautiful cherry blossom. A breeze loosened its delicate pink petals, which cascaded down on Thomas's windscreen.

The position gave him an excellent view of the front door, without being so close that he would draw attention to himself. He sat drinking coffee from a thermos and munching on a chocolate bar.

He'd walked around, changed clothes in a nearby shopping centre, ditched the gun there too, then circled back to the street where Reynolds lived and where Thomas had left his van that morning.

While Thomas sat there, he thought of his work for the organisation. The whole thing had begun nearly a year earlier when he ran a training course on cybercrime for a group of judges, barristers and solicitors. It was meant to give them a foundation for understanding high-tech cases that came before them.

That training session changed Thomas's life. It was where he met Archie Browne, then a controversial Crown Court judge. Soon Archie would begin to call himself Imperator, and would set up Compenso, the organisation Thomas now worked for. Evidently, he was fond of Latin, *imperator* meaning something like "commander", and *compenso* translating as "I balance". At the training course, Archie had been an enthusiastic student, unusual for a man of his age and stature. Thomas had no idea then of the work they would do together.

A police constable startled Thomas by walking past the van's window. The man crossed the road, moving towards the Reynolds house.

Although Thomas had made it easy for them, he was impressed that the constable was already here. It was probably Reynolds's phone that had done it. They might not have found the wallet yet. Or maybe they recognised Reynolds when they looked at his body. He often appeared as one of those talking heads on BBC debates about the economy.

Thomas put the thermos down and watched transfixed as the constable knocked on Reynolds's door. The officer stared at his shoes while he waited to see if anyone was home.

The worst part of the job, Thomas was sure. Notifying next of kin of a death. Watching it was a bittersweet moment for Thomas.

Brook Reynolds's wife opened the door. Dr. Reynolds's lips tightened at the sight of a constable, whose head stayed respectfully dipped, hands clutched together in front of him.

The constable was talking.

Talking.

Suddenly the wife doubled over like she'd been struck. An imploring look in her eyes. The constable, hands out, not touching her but ready to provide support if she fell.

As Dr. Reynolds cried on her doorstep, Thomas felt a stab of regret. This woman would never understand the kindness he had done her.

CHAPTER TEN

Dublin. Thursday, 8:39 pm.
Florence stormed into her apartment, flicked on the light and slammed the door behind her. The lovely fifth-floor penthouse, such a joy to her normally, felt dead and soulless.

She threw down her bag and stalked across the room to the window. The Dublin mountains reared up in the distance, a dark outline against the fading sky. At this moment, she hated the mountains, hated the air, hated everything.

It had been another nightmare taxi ride from the ramen bar. She'd tried to call her father but got no answer. She phoned him seven times before remembering that he was at an opera tonight with one of his friends, a prominent and very expensive solicitor.

Florence needed to talk to someone. Normally, she discussed her problems with Hazel, her best friend for so many years, and Simon was her other go-to listener.

Florence closed her eyes and sobbed.

She couldn't believe Hazel had stolen the love of her life. Nor that Simon had stolen her best friend and made her his partner.

A double betrayal, the worst Florence could imagine.

How had it happened?

Which of them started the affair?

Was there any innocent explanation? Florence didn't think so. If there was, Simon would have been able to explain. Instead, he had dumped her. It was obviously an admission of guilt. He'd cheated and he'd dumped her when she found out.

Florence wondered if Simon and Hazel were together now. They might be having acrobatic sex in Simon's bed right this second.

Florence continued to sob, until finally the tears dried up.

After a minute standing looking out over Dublin, she wiped her eyes. She needed to vent, but she couldn't think of anyone she could talk to about this. There was no one else she trusted, and it was killing her to keep her feelings bound up inside.

She brought her laptop over to the couch and powered it up, thinking vaguely that she might write an e-mail to one of her friends who she hadn't seen in a while. She began typing, then changed her mind. The problem was that she had been spending so much time with Simon, she'd paid no attention to anyone else. She could hardly send a message to someone she hadn't spoken to in ages, just so she could tell them about the end of her relationship.

She turned on the Wi-Fi and dug in the fridge looking for tonic water to go with her gin. Once she'd found it, she poured a glass and drank half of it at once.

She brought her drink to the couch, put the laptop in her lap and logged onto Facebook. For a whole minute she stared at Simon's profile.

How could she love him so much this morning and hate him so much now?

What had changed?

Only that she knew the truth.

She wanted other people to know too, to share her disgust. She started to write a post.

I found out the truth about Simon Hill today. He's NOT a nice guy. More like a cheating scumbag. We are SO over!

Florence paused to review what she'd written. No one reading it would feel sympathy for her. They'd only be amused at how easily she was misled. And the post would linger online forever. It would never go away. Future boyfriends – if Florence was dumb enough to date again – would be able to read these words. Clients might see the post too.

She deleted her words and logged out.

Florence's phone rang. Simon, calling at last? She grabbed the phone and checked the screen. It was Jill, her PA, again.

"Go away," she said, not answering. But the phone kept ringing. She gave in and answered. "What is it?"

"Hi, Florence. Is this a good time to talk?"

"No, it's not," Florence said.

"I'm so sorry," Jill said. "It's just that I had another e-mail from Jon Glynn."

"Who?"

"The guy you met earlier? You had that meeting with him? The one who's worried about his trade mark?"

All that work stuff felt like it had taken place a thousand years ago.

"Jill, it's late. Go home and stop pestering me."

Florence ended the call. She threw her phone on the couch beside her and turned her attention back to her laptop.

She brought up Google and typed *I hate my boyfriend* into the search bar. Most of the results were relationship articles in women's magazines. She clicked on a few of them, but found nothing interesting, so she continued to scroll down the search results. At the bottom of the page, she saw a listing for a website called Better Confess.

Florence clicked on the link. The website was simple. There were no images, just black writing on a white background. The website seemed to be a place for people to anonymously confess to shameful things they had thought and done. The confessions were arranged into categories, based on the seven deadly sins: pride, greed, lust, envy, gluttony, wrath and sloth.

Florence clicked on *Gluttony*.

A list of titles appeared. Florence clicked on the first one, which was called *Chicken*. The text of the anonymous confession appeared on the screen. Florence read the words of a man who had binged on an entire chicken. It was meant to feed his family for dinner, but the guy arrived home from work early. He ate the whole bird before his wife and children got home.

I don't know why I did it. I feel so stupid, he wrote.

Florence shook her head in amazement. She finished her gin and tonic. Someone had left a comment below the confession. *Don't be too hard on yourself. Try to do better next time.*

Florence broke out laughing.

"Yeah, try not to eat a chicken next time," she sneered.

Florence fixed herself another drink. While she was on her feet, she called a nearby take-away and ordered some food.

Then she sat back down in front of the laptop and scrolled through more of the confessions. Some were funny, some stupid, others disturbing. It was amazing what awful things people could do.

Simon should use this website, Florence thought. *Hazel, too. They should confess what they did to me.*

Then Florence had another idea. *She* could vent her feelings here. No one would ever know it was her. And the rage that gripped her demanded some kind of release. Maybe she'd feel better afterwards, if she knew people understood her pain.

At the top of the page, there was a button with the word *CONFESS.* Florence clicked on it. The website didn't ask her to log in or create an account and for that she was grateful. It took her straight to a form. At the top, there was a choice of which category the confession belonged in. Beneath that was a line to insert the title of the confession, and there was a large box underneath, where the confession itself could be written.

Florence clicked on the category *Wrath*, and titled her confession, *Dead Boyfriend.*

Then she moved onto the confession box.

She began typing.

My boyfriend cheated on me with my best friend. I really hate him and I really hate her. Honestly, I feel like killing my boyfriend. I wish he was dead.

CHAPTER ELEVEN

Dublin, Thursday, 8:50 pm.
Simon Hill took a stool at the bar. He was still in the city centre. After storming out of the ramen bar, he'd walked aimlessly until he found himself at the door of this pub. It was loud and almost full. Groups of men with pints stood watching a football game, which boomed from a TV on the other side of the lounge.

That's it, Simon thought. *I can't do it anymore.*

Florence was impossible. And he'd nearly married her. He rested his hands on the long wooden bar.

"Help you?"

A bored-looking barman stood in front of him.

Simon had sworn to himself that he'd never end up in this situation again. Sitting alone in a bar.

"Guinness," he said.

The barman turned away without a word and began to fill a pint glass, then set it down to settle under the tap.

So much for promises.

Simon's phone buzzed. It was a text from Hazel.

What did she say?

Simon sighed. Of course, Hazel knew he'd been about to propose, as did a few close friends and his parents. Now he was going to have to tell them it was off. His mother would be pleased. She'd given him a look when he told her his plan. At the time, he'd felt irritated that she wasn't happy for him. But maybe she'd been more right than he knew.

A glistening pint of Guinness appeared in front of him. Simon tapped his card on the payment device, nodded to the barman.

Another buzz in his pocket.

Hazel again.

She said yes, right? Don't keep me in suspense.

Simon tapped out a reply.

It's off.

Then he took a sip of stout.

He felt the bulge in his pocket. The stupid ring was still there. He'd have to go back to the shop the next day to get a refund. That was going to be a fucking delight.

He took a long sip, draining a third of the glass. A pleasant buzz filled his head. It had been so long since he'd that feeling.

His phone rang. It would have been nice to ignore it, but Hazel was the kind of person who'd call him until he picked up.

She said, "What do you mean, it's off? Don't tell me she said no?"

Simon sighed. "I didn't propose. We split up."

A pause.

"Where are you?"

"Nowhere," Simon said.

"What's that noise in the background?"

"A soccer game. I'm in a bar."

"Are you crazy? What are you doing?"

Simon took another long drag on his glass.

"What?" he said. "I'm just having one drink."

"You're an alcoholic, Simon," she said. "You can't have just one drink."

"Let's see."

"Tell me where you are. I'm going to come and get you."

He told her. As soon as he was off the phone, he ordered another drink.

CHAPTER TWELVE

London. Thursday, 8:55 pm.

The house in East Sheen which Thomas Ogden shared with his wife and son was a lovely three-bed affair with bay windows and a converted attic. They'd moved here when Thomas was promoted to a more senior position in the penetration testing division of the cybersecurity company where he worked.

Thomas's pulse was still racing when he parked in the driveway. The image of Brook Reynolds collapsing with a hole in his head kept replaying in his mind. The breath that came from the man's mouth as he died. The soft bump of his head as it hit the tarmac of the Central Avenue.

Everything had gone well and Thomas had completed the job within twenty hours of receiving the order. Four hours to spare. Another assignment successfully completed.

Most people had the wrong idea about Thomas. He knew that his colleagues thought him shy and nerdy. They would have been surprised to see the reality – that he had a rich and happy home life, that he liked nothing more than a full day of hiking in the mountains with Wendy and Freddy. But that reality was none of their business.

He got out of the van, and waved a greeting to Agnes, an elderly neighbour, who was examining the tomato plants in her front garden. She waved back, glad as always to see her helpful young neighbour.

As he approached the door of the house, Thomas glanced around. Years of stalking others had made him hypersensitive to his own vulnerabilities. As always, he had been careful to make sure he wasn't followed home. Eternal vigilance. That was the watchword for survival.

As soon as he opened the door, Freddy came running.

"Daddy's home," the boy shouted and threw his arms around Thomas's knees. Thomas ruffled his nine-year-old's hair.

"Alright buddy? Why are you still up?"

"Mum let me wait up so I could say good night," Freddy said.

"Is that right?"

Their German Shepherd, Max, came running down the hall next. He jumped up on Thomas, his sharp nails digging into Thomas's belly.

Thomas patted him, then sat down on the stool inside the door. This shoe-changing area was a recent innovation. Wendy had placed a shoe rack and a stool next to the door, and bought a pair of slippers for each member of the family. It had seemed like a silly idea to Thomas. But a month later, leaving outdoor shoes at the door had become the new normal.

He slipped off his shoes, replacing them with his slippers. They reminded him of his grandfather, a hard-working miner from Wales who only softened enough to wear slippers when he turned eighty. As always, Max took the opportunity to shower Thomas with kisses while Thomas had his head low. Thomas squeezed his eyes shut and laughed.

"Get away, Max." Thomas got to his feet and hung his jacket on the rack. "Where's your mum?"

Freddy shrugged. "I don't know. Can we play PlayStation?"

"I'm here," Wendy called from the kitchen.

Thomas followed the sound of her voice. She was putting a plate of lasagne in the microwave. Even in the subdued lighting of the kitchen, her hair glowed like autumn leaves. As usual, her smile lifted his spirits.

"So late," Wendy said. "I take it you didn't eat?"

"No." Thomas had been too excited to think about food, except for the bar of chocolate with his coffee. That had held off his appetite until now.

"You stay late at the office so often. They better give you a raise."

Thomas smiled. "I don't mind."

He leaned in for a kiss, but Wendy stepped out of reach.

"Wash your face," she said. "I saw Max drooling all over you."

After splashing some water on his hands and face at the sink, Thomas sat down at the kitchen table to eat his dinner. Freddy chased Max around the table until he got dizzy. It was pleasant to catch up with them. After a while, Wendy put Freddy to bed.

While she was upstairs, Thomas washed the dishes, and left some jasmine green tea steeping in boiling water. Then he went upstairs to read Freddy a bedtime story, but his son was already asleep. Thomas just stood over the bed and watched him for a while.

Precious moments, he thought. The boy was growing up fast. Soon the childish innocence would be chipped away. Freddy would see how corrupt the world really was.

Thomas made his way back downstairs and lifted the tea out of the water. He took a sip as Wendy hugged him from behind.

"Want to look at something on Neflix?" she said.

"Could do," Thomas said slowly.

"Don't tell me you want to work."

"Just for five minutes," he said. "Do you mind?"

Wendy released him, put her hands on her hips. "I have to be up early for work. Can't we spend time together anymore?"

"Of course. You get Netflix ready. By the time you've chosen something to watch, I'll be on the couch, okay?"

"Fine," Wendy said. She added, "You better make me a nice mojito."

He gave her a kiss and made his way upstairs to the study. He closed the door, locked it, and powered up his laptop.

Thomas usually savoured the feeling of satisfaction for a few days after he completed a job.

Even a few weeks. But tonight, he was impatient to start again, to do another job.

Was that a bad sign? He couldn't afford to let the work become emotional. Everything had to be done with clinical precision.

He brought up his favourite hunting ground, Better Confess. The most violent desires could usually be found in the section entitled Wrath, so he didn't waste time browsing the others. Yet even in this category, a lot of the confessions were mundane. People confessing to road rage or venting about a co-worker. Good people who felt bad about little things.

Then he noticed a confession called *Dead Boyfriend*. The title grabbed his attention. He clicked on it.

My boyfriend cheated on me with my best friend. I really hate him and I really hate her. Honestly, I feel like killing my boyfriend. I wish he was dead.

Thomas smiled. This could be promising. He typed out a reply and powered down the laptop just as Wendy called his name.

"Coming," he said.

CHAPTER THIRTEEN

Dublin. Thursday, 9:00 pm.

Hazel pushed through the doors of the pub. Her brief conversation with Simon had alarmed her and left her with questions. Florence could be difficult, but what had made Simon change his mind about something as important as asking her to marry him? Hazel knew how important marriage was to Simon and his family, devoted Catholics who went to church every week.

While talking to Simon, Hazel had been in a shoe shop where she had gone to find something to wear to Ronan's party. She wanted something with a high heel. Something that would look good with the dress she got at the weekend.

She'd managed to find a pair that were just what she had been looking for. Cream coloured and high, they made her legs look longer and slimmer. After talking to Simon, she'd paid for the shoes, then hurried to the pub.

Noise and the smell of beer hit her just inside the door. Football on the TV, rowdy men with beer guts and pints. Simon sat on a stool at the bar, his head down, eyes narrowed. His hand was wrapped around a half-full pint.

Hazel made her way across the lounge, noticing that Simon looked like a different person to the man she had been laughing with just a short time earlier in the evening. Where was the optimistic young man who'd picked out an engagement ring? The person in front of her looked older, defeated.

"What are you doing?"

Simon looked up when Hazel spoke, but his eyes quickly went back to his drink.

"Hello Hazel."

He took a long sip of Guinness.

Unbelievable.

Hazel watched him. She remembered the period before Simon met Florence. He'd been at a low ebb, and Hazel had been the one who convinced him to attend his first AA meeting. Even went to the door with him and waited outside until the meeting ended, to make sure he didn't bail. Going there had changed his life.

Hazel sensed that whatever had happened with Florence was big. Enough to really knock him off course.

"Simon, stop."

He patted the stool beside him. "What will you have?" he said. He waved a hand to get the barman's attention.

"I'm not drinking anything, and neither are you."

As the barman came over, Simon reached for his pint again, about to drain the last of the stout. Hazel grabbed it first. She emptied the contents out on the floor.

"Hey, hey, hey," said the barman. "Out, you two."

"We're going," Hazel said.

"Like hell we are," Simon said. "Give me another pint."

A shake of the head from the barman.

Hazel took Simon's elbow. "Come on."

Reluctantly, he slipped off his stool. Normally so sharp, Simon looked sad and dishevelled. A strand of black hair had hung across his eyes. He put on his coat and tapped his coat pocket. Hazel guided him to the door, afraid to let him out of her sight.

CHAPTER FOURTEEN

Dublin. Thursday, 9:15 pm.
A tall, young man delivered Florence's pizza. She stepped out of the elevator and walked across the lobby of the apartment building to him. His face was dour, his eyes sleepy, in contrast to the brightness of his blue and red uniform.

How dare he look bored? He was bored waiting a whole minute for her to come downstairs? That was nothing. She'd waited *ages* for her order to come and, in the meantime, had become roaring drunk.

She unlocked the front door and accepted the pizza box, and the bag containing chicken wings, chips and Coke. If Florence had been hungry when she ordered, she was famished now. The delivery guy didn't budge after handing her the food.

Florence said, "What are you waiting for? Don't expect a tip after being so slow."

She slammed the door in his face and cackled to herself. The tonic had run out long ago, but she still had gin. Now she could mix it with Coke.

She ate a few chips as she rode the elevator back upstairs.

Once inside her apartment, she shut the door and placed all the food on the kitchen table. There was more than she had expected. She made a good stab at finishing everything, all the same, managing three quarters.

As she finished eating, her phone rang. It was her father.

"Daddy, hello-dee-ho?"

She could hear traffic sounds in the background. Then his warm, responsible voice came over the phone's speaker, reassuring as ever. But his tone was sharp.

"Florence? Are you drunk?"

"I'm as sober sass a sailor, Daddy."

He sighed. "Dear, you're slurring your words."

"Oh, I just had a little dlink. How was the popera?"

"Fine, dear. Listen—"

"I always listen to you Daddy!"

"Then listen to me now. Drink a glass of water and go to bed."

"I want to talk—"

"We can talk tomorrow, when you're in a fit state. You are at home now, aren't you?"

"Yes, I am."

"Thank goodness for that. Go to bed now, dear. Okay? Good night."

"But Daddy—"

The line went dead.

"Huh," Florence muttered.

She fixed herself a gin and Coke, then returned to the couch. After posting her confession, she'd been browsing other people's posts.

She went to the section of the website titled *Wrath* and looked through the confessions until she found her own one. *Dead Boyfriend.* She read through it.

"Simon, you are a terrible person and I hate you," Florence muttered.

She was surprised to see a comment under her confession. Like all the posts on the site, it was anonymous.

I can take care of him for you.

"I wish," Florence said. She took a slug of her drink. After a moment, she realised she could reply.

She wrote, *Yeah, take him out, man! I want him to shit his pants!!!! LOL.*

A new comment appeared when she refreshed the page. It was a weird-looking e-mail address with a long string of numbers.

Florence copied the address into her own e-mail account and wrote a message.

It was short.

Only two words.

But it would change her life.

CHAPTER FIFTEEN

Dublin. Thursday, 9:31 pm.

Simon gazed at the strawberry milkshake in front of him. He and Hazel were sitting in an American-style diner with vinyl booths. Elvis was playing on a bubble jukebox. The milkshakes came in stainless steel shakers. They must have been a litre if they were a drop. Half the shake was poured out into a glass, set in a steel holder with a steel handle.

"I'm starving," Hazel said.

The smell of fried beef from the grill was beginning to get to Simon too. They'd both ordered burgers. Hazel had opted for a pineapple and chilli topping, a combination that made Simon want to gag. He'd chosen bacon and cheese.

Their table was halfway down the length of the diner. Next to them was a line of stools along the counter. Behind that, the fry cook tended to their patties.

Simon took a sip of his milkshake. He was a milkshake aficionado, and reserved different flavours for particular occasions. This was definitely a strawberry moment.

He patted his coat pocket again. He'd spent two months' wages on the ring, as he'd heard that was a rule of thumb when it came to engagement rings.

"Are you going to tell me what happened with Florence?" Hazel said.

She was looking at him over her own milkshake – chocolate flavour. Simon reserved chocolate for his birthday.

Simon sighed. "I can't take it."

"What?"

"Her tantrums. Her bad temper. Her thoughtlessness. I thought she'd grow out of all that."

Hazel said, "You know Florence has a good heart."

"She saw you and me."

"What?"

"She must have passed by when we were coming out of the jewellery shop."

Hazel nodded slowly.

"And?"

"She saw us hug."

"Oh."

"Yeah, oh. She saw us together and immediately jumped to the conclusion that I must be cheating on her." Simon laughed a humourless laugh. "Can you believe that?"

Hazel took another sip of milkshake while she gathered her thoughts.

"Okay, so she had a tantrum?"

"Yep. Just about wrecked the restaurant. Breaking glasses, shouting at waiters, making a scene."

Simon shook his head.

"She'll calm down. You know she goes nuclear sometimes."

"All too well." Simon jabbed a finger in Hazel's face. "Florence goes nuclear every time something doesn't go her way. How can you marry someone like that?"

"Take a breath, Simon." Hazel was smiling now, as if he was being silly. She said, "Did you explain to her?"

Simon shrugged. "What's the point? She never listens anyway. And even if she did, so what? Tomorrow she'd find something else to get mad about."

"So send her a bouquet of flowers."

Simon said, "I've done that a hundred times. No more flowers, no more apologies."

"Simon—"

"Do you know," he interrupted, "how many times she's dumped me? At least fifty times this year."

"Come on."

"No kidding. I'm done."

A waitress in 50's diner garb appeared with their burgers and two portions of French fries. Her badge read, *Margie.* She looked like she'd been tending tables for more years than she wanted to count, but she had a kind smile and Simon immediately warmed to her.

She said, "Here you are, folks. Enjoy."

"Thanks," Hazel said.

Simon pulled his burger towards him. He knew Florence would never be caught dead in a place like this. She'd look down her nose at a woman like Margie.

Simon said, "I give up. No more Florence."

CHAPTER SIXTEEN

London. Thursday, 9:33 pm.
In the kitchen, Thomas Ogden washed Wendy's mojito glass and his own mug, which was caked with dried cocoa, now tough as cement. Wendy said the cocktail tasted like heaven, not too sweet, and plenty tangy, but she'd kept glancing at Thomas while they watched the movie. His wife always noticed when he was distracted.

Wendy had picked a romantic comedy and two of them had snuggled up on the couch to watch it. Thomas did his best to concentrate but he was eager to check whether he'd got a response to the comment he left on Better Confess.

After forty-five minutes, Wendy stopped the movie.

"You don't like it," she said.

Thomas thought about lying, but he preferred not to. "It's not that. I'm just thinking about work."

"You need to turn off once in a while."

Thomas heard the exasperation in his wife's voice.

"You're completely right. Sorry."

Wendy hadn't exactly stormed off, as she rarely did anything as violent as that, but she had left him sitting on the couch alone.

Now she was in the bathroom. Thomas heard the water begin to flow as Wendy took a shower.

Perfect.

He hurried upstairs to the study, where he stuck a USB stick into the laptop and booted up TAILS. It was a security-focused operating system that could be run directly from a flash drive. It was completely anonymous and left no trace on the computer on which it was being run. All traffic went through the TOR Network, and TAILS came with Pidgin, an excellent encrypted messaging app. These were some of the reasons it had become Thomas's favourite operating system.

He got onto Better Confess and saw the reply.

Yeah, take him out, man! I want him to shit his pants!!!! LOL.

The person sounded drunk or stupid or both, but that was no reason to hold back. A quiver of excitement passed through Thomas.

He sent a message to Archie and provided the link to the post. *I found a possible client on Better Confess. I want this, if they decide to proceed.*

It was irregular to go hunting business. It usually came to the organisation by itself. Then Archie assigned the case to an operative. But sometimes you had to be active.

That was what Archie had said the second time Thomas met him, before he had dubbed himself Imperator. It was months after the cybersecurity training Thomas had given. By then, Archie had been stripped of his position as a judge. He was an outcast, a pariah shouting about injustice, this time the injustice he had suffered himself.

Thomas had run into him in a bar in Mayfair one night. Archie would have been easily recognizable, even if he hadn't been flamboyantly wearing a red velvet jacket and the crispest white shirt Thomas had ever seen. Archie's handsome dark skin, fading red hair, freckles and piercing blue eyes were an arresting combination. Thomas took the stool next to him, they got talking and they didn't stop until 4 am.

Wendy was furious when he got home, but even then, groggy and hoarse from talking, Thomas had known that the conversation with Archie Browne would change his life. And it did. They'd been working together ever since.

Thomas's phone rang. The call was being run through a darknet app that allowed for completely anonymous contact. Of course it had been Thomas's idea. That was why Archie needed him. Archie's own idea had been to use WhatsApp to communicate.

"Isn't that secure enough? It's encrypted," he'd said to Thomas with a note of exasperation.

"Can you prove it?" had been Thomas's reply.

Although WhatsApp was presented as being encrypted end-to-end, users could not inspect the code behind the app to verify that this was true. They had to take it on trust that Facebook, WhatsApp's owner, was not accessing their calls and messages. Thomas trusted few people. He certainly didn't trust Facebook. Thankfully he did not need to. And he'd persuaded Archie to use a different service.

When Thomas answered the call, a distorted voice spoke.

"Fiat justitia…"

Let justice be done…

Thomas completed the Latin phrase. "… ruat caelum."

… though the heavens fall.

It was their customary greeting, part of the pomp that Archie insisted on once he became Imperator. Thomas's own voice would also be digitally distorted, so he'd sound the same to Archie on the other end of the line.

Archie said, "I have considered the post on Better Confess. The confessor might be venting, although it is possible they are serious. I have posted a link to a temporary disposable e-mail address. Let us see if they bite."

"Alright."

Archie liked to use the e-mail accounts you could set up in seconds, use once, and which were then deleted within an hour, obliterating all data in the account. They were relatively easy to hack, but they'd mostly likely have auto-destructed before anyone tried to gain access. Thomas generally avoided them himself.

"Are you sure you want the job, if it goes ahead?" Archie said. "You completed an assignment today. I have another operative who could handle this."

Thomas wondered exactly how many operatives Imperator had now. He'd been getting cagier and cagier as the months went by and the bodies piled up. Didn't he trust Thomas anymore?

"I'm ready to play again."

"This is not a game."

Thomas heard the shower stop. Wendy would finish in the bathroom soon. She'd dry herself, brush her teeth, apply moisturiser and then do her pre-bed stretches. There wasn't a lot of time.

"I know," Thomas whispered. "But I'm the best. And I'm available."

There was a long pause.

"Let us see if they bite," the distorted voice said finally, and the line went dead.

Thomas waited in the dimly lit room, hoping he would be the one to be assigned this job. The money could buy them a nice holiday when summer came around.

He'd thought of taking care of jobs on his own but had held off doing it. Archie had shown himself to be useful, managing the flow of information, money and weapons. On the Brook Reynolds job, for example, he had arranged for the provision of the gun and silencer. And he had a source on the Metropolitan Police, which could be valuable.

After a few minutes, an e-mail arrived. Just two words.

What next?

Thomas grinned. The words were from the person on Better Confess. They had e-mailed Archie and Archie had forwarded the e-mail to Thomas.

Which meant that the job was his.

CHAPTER SEVENTEEN

Dublin. Thursday, 10:01 pm.

Hazel drove Simon home. He sat in the passenger seat, the streetlights passing over his face, as they moved through the city. Simon's thirst seemed to have been slaked by the milkshake in the diner. Hopefully the food helped to take his mind off booze. Hazel didn't want to see him backslide. If she left him to go home alone, he might end up in another bar, drinking himself to oblivion. That would do no one any good.

Aside from anything else, Hazel and Simon were both attending Ronan O'Brien's party the following afternoon.

Ronan was a jolly bear of a man who had been their manager at Transcend Promotions for years. His wife, Deb, was a Detective Garda and she had been transferred to Claremorris, in the west of the country, a year earlier. So the couple had had to sell their home in Dublin and move. The birthday party would be the first time Simon and Hazel seen Ronan since he left. Ronan had booked rooms for some of his friends in a hotel for the next night. He was a party animal so Hazel was sure the celebrations would go on all night.

Simon was quiet. Hazel wondered if he was thinking about how he'd have to go to the party alone.

Hazel said, "Maybe you can give Florence a call tonight?"

Simon shook his head. "Not a chance."

"You'll wait till morning?"

"No. I told you, I'm done. That's it."

"For real?" Hazel registered the stony expression on his face.

"For real. It's not first time I've thought of ending things."

"Give her another chance."

"No," Simon said, and there was absolute certainty in his voice. "That's it. The very last time. Florence and I are over."

"It will devastate her."

"It's no picnic for me either." Simon was silent for a moment. Then he said, "I hope your dating life is going better than mine. What's the current guy's name? Larry? Harry?"

Hazel laughed. "Gary."

"Right. He's coming tomorrow, isn't he?"

Gary was a pro-golfer Hazel had met on the ninth green at her club. She had only gone out with him for a few months. Aside from tips on her swing, it turned out they had very little to talk about.

"Alas poor Gary didn't make the grade. I'll be on my own tomorrow too."

"Sorry to hear that."

Hazel smiled. "No big deal. He was kind of boring."

Simon said, "Now I have to think about dating again. I mean, not now, but some day. And I'll have to get in shape and pretend to be interesting. All that hell."

Simon's apartment complex appeared ahead. Hazel turned into the car park.

"Are you kidding me?" Hazel said. "You have no idea what a catch you are."

"Not according to Florence."

Hazel brought the car to a stop in front of the building. She put on the handbrake and looked at Simon.

"I'm sure Florence values you enormously, deep down."

"Whatever. It doesn't matter."

"You don't mean that."

"Oh, I do."

She looked up at the building. She knew his apartment was on the third floor, but she'd never been up there.

"What are you going to do now?" Hazel asked.

Simon shrugged.

"Maybe do a workout."

"That would be good if your stomach wasn't full."

Simon rubbed his eyes.

"True. Then maybe I'll just have a shower and think about killing myself." Simon smiled to show he was joking. "Thanks for getting me out of that pub.

You were right. That's a path I don't want to go down again."

"I don't want to see you go down it either."

Simon reached for the door handle. He hesitated, then said, "Do you want to come up?"

Hazel hadn't intended to, but maybe she should. It would be no harm to make sure he really went home and didn't wander off down the street to a pub instead.

"Just for a minute," Hazel said.

CHAPTER EIGHTEEN

Dublin. Thursday, 10:15 pm.
Sluggish from all the food she'd guzzled, Florence browsed videos on YouTube until she received an e-mail. It came from a different address, but she was sure it was from the same people. The e-mail contained two links and a message.

Download the TOR Browser. You need to use this for your security and anonymity. When you have installed it, copy the second link into it. We are Compenso. Find us.

TOR? Compenso? The message was almost enough to give Florence a headache.

But she clicked on the link and waited for the browser to download. Like she didn't have enough of them. Her desktop was cluttered with Chrome, Firefox and Edge. The program downloaded and an icon appeared.

Florence opened the new browser. It showed her what her IP address appeared to be. A button on the top left showed her three nodes around which her signal was being bounced before reaching the TOR Network. So this was how people browsed the web anonymously. Suddenly Florence felt excited.

She copied and pasted the second link into the TOR Browser. The link looked strange and it ended in .onion. The link brought her directly to some kind of store. At first glance, it looked much like any online shop. But then she began to notice exactly what kind of goods it sold. There were no books here. No food. No fashion. It was all about drugs, weapons, and bundles of credit card numbers.

She couldn't see Compenso listed. But she did see a "services" section, which she clicked on. Within it, there were sex workers, hackers and "muscle". She clicked through to the muscle section and saw a variety of vendors listed. One of them was labelled Compenso. There was a star-rating system on the site, and Compenso's rating was 4.7 out of 5 based on 6 customer reviews.

Florence burst out laughing.

Customer reviews?

It's a joke, she thought. *They must be actors or something, who go and scare people for you.*

She read the description of the business.

Compenso offers a professional elimination service. The job will be completed within 24 hours of an order being placed (applies to UK and Ireland only).

There was an *Enquire* button. She clicked on it and a chat box opened.

She typed, *Hi! This is the person who wrote Dead Boyfriend.*

She sipped her drink and waited a moment.

Typing… the screen said. A message appeared. *Are you serious about this?*

Serious as hell, Florence typed. *I want you to make him pay.*

You're going to have to do a few things.

Like what?

The person on the other end gave her a bitcoin receiving address. This was how Compenso wanted to be paid. And they gave her instructions on how to get a bitcoin wallet, how to use a bitcoin exchange to turn real money into bitcoin, how to use a cryptocurrency tumbler to keep things anonymous, and a bunch of other stuff that made her head hurt.

Florence pressed on because she needed to pay immediately. If she paid, Compenso would do its part within twenty-four hours.

Guaranteed.

Florence thought of Simon being terrified by the appearance of a mysterious stranger. Her vision was slightly blurry, but she was in a boisterous mood now. She didn't want the fun to stop.

"Okay," Florence told herself. "Let's focus. I need booze."

She went to the kitchen and fixed herself another drink. Then she returned to the laptop and followed the step-by-step instructions to complete the payment. She was too drunk to bother figuring out how much it cost in real money. In any case, they only wanted half the amount now.

The whole thing was tedious but relatively easy because of Compenso's detailed instructions. Soon the bitcoin had been transferred. Then she got a message.

What's your boyfriend's name?

Simon Hill, she wrote back.

Okay. Give us a photo of him, his home address, and his place of employment.

Florence did. Then she wrote, *What's the best way to kill someone?*

The professional way is to go up behind them when they are on their doorstep, and shoot them in the back of the head twice.

Florence broke out laughing at this reply. The professional way. They sounded so serious.

Cackling, she slammed her laptop shut and went looking for her phone. Eventually she found it in the fridge. Still laughing, she rang Simon but got no answer. When the call went to voicemail, Florence laughed down the line and said, "The joke's on you, Simon. You're dead."

After hanging up, she lay down on the couch and passed out.

CHAPTER NINETEEN

Dublin. Thursday, 10:20 pm.

Simon flicked on the lights. Hazel followed him inside the apartment. Though they'd known each other for years, she'd never been inside his home. And he'd only moved into this place six months earlier.

The entrance hallway led into a sprawling sitting room. It had lots of space, and everything was white and sterile, with big floor-to-ceiling windows. It looked like a bit like a dental surgery.

"Home sweet home," Simon said, dropping his keys on the glass coffee table.

"It's similar to Florence's place," Hazel said. "The white walls, white shelves, white couches."

Simon slumped on the nearest couch.

"Bingo. She said I needed a suitable apartment. I can barely afford it though."

Hazel said, "Maybe she thought you'd ask her to move in here with you."

Simon cocked an eyebrow. "Really? You think she expected that?"

"I don't know," she said. "But I wonder."

He snorted. "Well, that's not going to happen."

Hazel went back out to the hallway. Simon heard her pottering around in the kitchen on the other side of the hall.

"What are you doing?" Simon said.

She didn't answer right away. But he heard her opening the fridge and the cupboards. He slumped on the couch and closed his eyes. He heard her come back into the room a moment later.

"Just checking you don't have a stash of booze."

Simon laughed bitterly.

"Nope," he said. "Not a drop. I didn't know I'd need it."

Hazel walked around the back of the couch. She dropped her hands to Simon's shoulders. Her fingers felt cool through his shirt.

"You don't need it."

She grabbed his throat and pretended to throttle him. They both laughed.

"I guess I'm to blame," Hazel said, letting go of him. Simon opened his eyes, and watched Hazel as she made her way around the couch.

"For what?" he said, moving his coat so she could sit down next to him.

"I played matchmaker for you two."

"Oh, yeah."

Simon laughed. Neither of them spoke for a while. Simon looked up at Hazel shyly.

"Can I tell you something?"

"What?"

"That time, when you set me up with Florence… I was actually working up the courage to ask *you* out."

"Really?"

"Dumb, right? I know I'm not your type, but I kind of had a crush on you."

"You never said anything."

Simon shrugged. "You would have turned me down."

"How do you know?"

Again, he shrugged.

"Well, you're home, and there's no alcohol in the place, so I guess I should go," she said. "I want to pack a bag for the trip tomorrow."

It would take more than two and a half hours to drive to Claremorris. She and Simon had both arranged to leave work in the middle of the afternoon.

"Could you stay?" Simon said. "Just a little longer."

Hazel hesitated.

"Okay," she said. "But I need a coffee."

"I can take care of that."

Simon decided he'd have a cup too, thinking it might help clear his mind. He made his way to the kitchen, where he turned on his coffee machine and waited as dark liquid started dripping into the pot.

He leaned his head against the cupboard and closed his eyes. The beers had made him sleepy and dull but that was nothing compared to the day's emotional turmoil.

He thought he'd be celebrating his engagement at this very moment. Instead, there was a Florenceshaped hole in his life. Here he was in an apartment she'd wanted him to rent, wearing clothes she had pushed him to pick. He couldn't believe he'd been such an idiot, going along with whatever Florence said. All for nothing.

Hazel's voice came from the sitting room. "Did you fall asleep in there?"

"Almost," Simon called back.

He poured two cups and brought them to the sitting room. Hazel was standing in front of his bookshelf, leafing through a Dan Brown novel.

"Have you read this one?"

"Sure, but Florence thinks books are a waste of time," Simon said.

Hazel smiled, returned the book to its shelf. "You know she has a short attention span."

"Short temper too."

He handed Hazel her coffee. His fingers grazed hers as she took the cup.

"Was Larry a reader?"

"Who?"

"Your last boyfriend."

"You mean Gary?" Hazel laughed. "No. It was one of the things I didn't like about him."

Simon sat down, but Hazel remained standing.

"I'm sorry I said that stuff," Simon said. "About having a crush on you. I didn't mean to make things weird."

"No, you didn't."

Just then his phone rang. "Florence," Simon said. He shook his head and returned the phone to his pocket. He had no idea what to say and he just sat there until Hazel broke the silence.

"Where's your bathroom?" she asked.

"Just down the hall on the left."

She finished her coffee, set down her cup and walked out of the room. Simon heard the bathroom door close and the fan come on. His phone beeped. He'd received a message saying Florence had left voicemail. Simon was about to listen to it when Hazel appeared in the doorway.

"I'm going to go," she said. "Are you okay?"

"Yeah, absolutely." Simon jumped to his feet. "Thanks for coming."

He followed her down the hall. At the front door, she stopped.

"So we're good for tomorrow?" Hazel said.

It took Simon a moment to remember what she was talking about. All because of the stupid beer. Literally. He felt stupid after drinking it.

Of course. The party.

"I guess."

"Don't guess."

"Right. I'm good."

Hazel hugged Simon. Slowly, she pulled away, pausing when her lips were right in front of his, almost but not quite touching. Hazel didn't kiss him. Just stared into his eyes, as if looking for something. Being so close to her, being uncertain what would happen – it sent an electric shiver down Simon's spine.

"Good night, Simon."

Hazel turned and walked down the corridor, disappearing into the stairwell. Simon closed the door and leaned against it while his pulse slowed.

Whoa. What just happened?

Simon didn't know. Something weird, anyway. He walked back over to the couch and slumped in it. Then he checked Florence's voice message.

"The joke's on you, Simon. You're dead."

CHAPTER TWENTY

London. Thursday, 11:11 pm.
Thomas had been patient with the client as he helped her pay in bitcoin. Over recent months he'd written a detailed set of instructions on the procedure, which he now provided to clients in a pdf document. Of course, the file also contained some malicious code that let Thomas have complete control over the client's computer. Why not? This client had asked for clarification a few times, so Thomas had been standing by his laptop.

He was sure that before tonight the woman had never visited the dark web. She probably thought she was anonymous now, thanks to the Tor Browser.

It wasn't true.

Though she was using the Tor Browser, her computer's operating system would still collect data on her. And it would leak data, as would other programs on her computer. But Thomas was not worried about that. He was satisfied that *he* was secure.

He received the details of the man she wanted killed. He was surprised to find that the job was in Ireland. Well, Dublin was only an hour away by plane, so it didn't matter.

Thomas had insisted that the client should pay extra so that the bitcoin transfer would happen as quickly as possible. She seemed a little outraged by that, but eventually she agreed. The bitcoin had hit Thomas's wallet at 10:44 pm. The job would have to be completed by the same time tomorrow, because of the twenty-four-hour guarantee.

Thomas had a lot of research to do.

Wendy's footsteps padded down the hall. She was doing her evening yoga so Thomas had a few more minutes.

He found a flight and booked it using his real name. He'd figure out some legitimate excuse for visiting Ireland. It was something he could think about tomorrow. No one was going to link him to the death of a complete stranger in another country. And he'd be back in London before the corpse got cold.

The plane departed from Heathrow at 10:25 am and arrived in Dublin at 11:30 am. That meant Thomas needed to get to Heathrow at about 9:30 am. He'd leave home at 8:30 am.

He tapped out an e-mail to his boss, explaining that he had an upset stomach and would not be able to come to work the next day.

Then he went to the bedroom. Thomas took a moment to pause in the doorway and watch Wendy stretching on her mat beside the bed. After a decade of marriage, his love for her remained undimmed.

"Are you going to have a shower?" Wendy asked, noticing him there.

"I love you," Thomas said.

Wendy shot him a suspicious look. "What's the bad news?"

"What?"

"You look like you're going to say something I don't want to hear."

Thomas laughed. As skilled as he was at lying, he had to be careful of Wendy. She knew him too well.

Thomas said. "I just got an e-mail from work. I have to go to a meeting in Dublin tomorrow."

"How long will you be gone?"

"Oh, I expect I'll be back tomorrow evening, or else first thing Saturday morning."

"This is crazy, Thomas. You're working all the time. I'm going to go into your office and tell them what I think of how they treat you."

"No, Wendy. Please don't."

"When will it end? When will they give me my husband back?"

She got to her feet and rolled up the mat. Then she slipped off her clothes and left them on a chair at the side of the room. Thomas admired her naked form as she searched in the bed for her pyjamas.

Love was the greatest force for good in the world, and the greatest force for bad, when it went wrong.

He said, "I'm sorry, but I promise, once this is over, I'm going to take a break."

"You always say that."

Wendy's face was scrunched tight. She pulled on her silky pyjamas. With his arms open, he went over to her. She ignored him and got under the duvet. Thomas belly-flopped on his side of the bed.

Still ignoring him, Wendy reached for her hardback copy of the Bible which sat on the bedside unit. The thing weighed about a tonne. Thomas had no idea how she held it up in bed, but she did, and she insisted on reading a passage every night. She said it kept nightmares away.

Wendy had an unbendable moral compass. It was one of the things that had attracted Thomas to her when they first met.

Thomas's own ethics were more fluid.

"Wendy, I know I've worked a lot lately and I'm sorry. But I'm going to make it up to you. Let's go away on holiday when this trip is over."

She looked at him over the top of her Bible.

"Are you sure you can get time off work?"

"I'll make it happen."

"Where would we go?"

"Anywhere you like. They're going to give me a bonus for all the overtime I've been doing."

Wendy returned to her Bible.

"Let's see," she said.

Thomas could see she was pleased. He said, "I'm going to pack a bag. I have to leave early."

He crawled up the bed. Wendy pretended not to see him. His head darted forward quickly as he tried to kiss her, but she was faster. She blocked him with the Bible and he ended up kissing the spine of the book.

CHAPTER TWENTY-ONE

Dublin. Friday, 7:58 am.

The next morning, Hazel arrived early at the office. She worked in a large open-plan room. Right now, it was empty. She set her pot of granola and yoghurt down on her desk and went to the kitchenette to make tea.

It would be a short day, because she would have to leave for Claremorris in the middle of the afternoon. She'd dressed a little more casual than usual, conscious of the travel that lay ahead. Stretch jeans and a soft white blouse. She'd packed a dress to wear in the evening, one with a slit up to her hip. It would go great with her new shoes.

She'd dreamt of Simon last night. He was taking her somewhere in his car. As he drove, he ran one hand through her hair and then began eating it.

Swallowing her hair.

He was so absorbed in it that he forgot about the road ahead.

Look out, she screamed, as a goat stepped in front of the car.

It was so weird.

Hazel powered up her computer and went online, checking a website she often consulted about the meaning of dreams. It said that the goat meant resilience, and the practice of eating hair was about doing something unpalatable.

Hazel munched on her granola while she thought. Hazel had set Florence up with Simon. She'd had no idea that Simon had a crush on her. If anything, she thought he'd be too clean and strait-laced to even think of her in such a way. He was such a nice, plain kind of guy. A little boring.

Footsteps behind her. Then Simon's voice.

"Morning."

Hazel turned, spoon in hand. Simon looked a little grim, but otherwise okay.

"You're early," she said.

"You too."

Hazel shrugged. "Have to leave early. Aren't you glad you're not hungover?"

Simon smiled faintly. "Yes, I am."

Perhaps they could both pretend last night hadn't happened. The final moments of the night, at least, when Hazel had almost kissed him. She'd felt sorry for Simon, and she'd been flattered to learn that he had secretly had a crush on her.

Simon took off his coat and hung it on the stand next to his desk. He patted his pocket.

"Is that the ring?" Hazel said.

"Yep."

"So you're going to ask her today? That's wonderful."

Simon scowled. He sat down at his desk, right opposite Hazel's, and fixed her with a level stare.

"No. I'm returning it to the shop at lunch time. I meant what I said last night. Florence and I are over."

Hazel didn't say anything. She had wondered if Simon and Florence would reconcile during the night. But no. Hazel should warn Florence. That's what a good friend would do. Maybe if Florence apologised, then Simon would reconsider ending things.

But Florence apologising was about as likely as another moon appearing in the night sky. As Simon took his seat, Hazel tried to remember the last time she'd heard an apology come out of Florence's mouth.

Nothing came to mind.

Hazel closed the tab on the dream psychology website.

"Did Ronan e-mail you about the hotel?" Simon asked.

"Yes. I have all the details."

Hazel knew she was in room 308. Simon was in 309. Of course, Hazel was meant to be going with Gary. And Simon was meant to be there with Florence. But now it would just be Hazel and Simon. If Florence found out, she'd be furious.

Simon said, "Ronan sent me a direct message on Twitter. A link to a million photos of the hotel. I have no idea what that was about. The place looks pretty average to me."

"You know Ronan. He enjoys life."

Simon grinned. "Yeah. Everything is perfect."

That was Ronan's favourite word. But Simon didn't feel there was anything perfect about today.

"I wonder why he didn't send me the link," Hazel said.

"Obviously I'm special," Simon said.

CHAPTER TWENTY-TWO

Dublin, Friday, 9:31 am.

Florence woke to find herself lying on the couch in her sitting room. She felt like a woodpecker had been hammering at her head all night. Her stomach was shrivelled up, and the stale taste of gin and Coke filled her mouth. She'd never be able to tolerate the flavour again for as long as she lived.

She sat up, her body aching from the awkward position she'd slept in, twisted half sideways, with one arm over her head. Somewhere, a phone was ringing. She felt around on the couch beneath her and found it. The screen said her father was calling.

Florence didn't want to talk to him – she wasn't sure she was capable of speech – but she answered anyway.

"Daddy?" Her voice was a croak.

"Florence, where are you?"

"At home."

"Why did you miss your nine o'clock meeting?"

What day is it, Friday? Yes, a client was due to come in at nine. Another one will be in at ten, and I'll miss that too.

"I have to go," Florence said.

She threw down the phone and ran to the bathroom, reaching it just in time to vomit onto the closed lid of the toilet.

She watched the mess drip onto the floor. In the mirror, her reflection looked absolutely awful. Yesterday's makeup was smeared clown-like across her face. Her eyes were bloodshot, her hair was astray, and the gap between her front teeth seemed to have grown even larger overnight.

Her phone beeped with a text message.

Daddy again, no doubt. He had little sympathy for employees with hangovers. She walked to the couch and checked the message.

No, not Daddy. It was from Simon.

A dull echo of the previous day's rage throbbed in Florence's heart.

Simon had cheated on her.

It would be best to delete the message unread. Don't even dignify his apology by reading it. Curiosity got the better of her, though, and she opened it.

Florence, I can't believe how little you trust me after our years together. I bought an engagement ring yesterday, because I planned to propose to you after dinner. Hazel helped me choose a ring. Yes, she kissed me – to congratulate me. I can't believe you would jump to the worst conclusion. Now I realise that you're not ready for marriage. I'm not sure you're even ready for a relationship. You're spoilt and irresponsible. Your voicemail reminds me of that. Anyway, I wish you all the best. I hope you're happy one day. It won't be with me.

Florence read the message three times. Her feelings changed from scorn to uncertainty to heartache.

Of course Simon had been about to propose. The truth was that she had expected as much for months. And *of course* Hazel would help him choose the right ring. She knew much more about jewellery than Simon, and she knew the kind of stuff Florence liked. The two friends often swapped earrings and bracelets, not to mention dresses and tops, both being size 10. And Hazel and Simon worked side-by-side so, of course, he would tell her what he was planning to do. It all made sense.

Another message arrived.

Simon: *I don't want to see you ever again.*

Florence hadn't known Simon had it in him to say something so sharp. To dump her by text message.

She threw the phone down on the couch and screamed as loud as she could, squeezing her fists tight and raising her face to the ceiling.

She tried to calm herself. What voicemail was Simon talking about? She struggled to remember. What did she say last night when she was drunk?

A terrible hint of a memory came back to her.

Florence had called Simon but hadn't got through to him. She remembered laughing down the line and saying, "The joke's on you, Simon. You're dead."

She shuddered at the memory, struggling to recall why she'd said that. What else did she do? Did she post something on Facebook?

She brought her laptop over to the table in her kitchen. The room was littered with the debris of the previous night. An open pizza box, with two slices left. A fruit fly flitted around the congealed ham. The smell of grease hung in the air.

Holding her breath, Florence cleaned off the table while her laptop powered up. She sat down and stared at the screen, surprised to find a new shortcut on her desktop.

Tor.

What was that?

Tor, Tor, Tor. She thought about it, her brain aching at the exertion. The Onion Router. The browser that let you browse the internet anonymously, bouncing your signal around the world to mask your real location.

Suddenly it all came back to her.

Better Confess and the darknet marketplace where she'd hired an assassin. Her pulse began to race.

Had she really done that?

She struggled to recollect whether it was all a joke. Had she asked for Simon to be scared or to be killed?

What had she been thinking? She didn't want anything to be done to Simon. He was the love of her life.

Florence opened her usual internet browser and logged onto her internet banking. Three thousand euro had been taken from her account.

"Oh my god," she whispered.

So that was the value of the bitcoin she'd purchased. And that was how much Compenso charged to kill somebody. Or that was half of it. She vaguely remembered the hitman saying that he charged half before and half after the job was complete.

She opened the Tor Browser and brought up the darknet marketplace where she'd found Compenso. There was a client login. Florence looked around her apartment until she found a notebook with a barely legible username and password. She had no memory whatsoever of writing them down.

After logging in, she was brought to a client area. She clicked a button marked *SECURE CHAT*. The chat history from last night appeared. Florence read over it in horror. She had given the hitman Simon's name, address, workplace, phone number and e-mail address.

She began typing.

I'm sorry, there's been a mistake. I want to cancel the job.

She waited but nothing happened. Maybe the guy was asleep. While waiting for a reply, she went to the kitchen and got herself some paracetamol and a vitamin supplement. She knocked them back with a glass of water, a shudder of nausea running through her.

A message was waiting when she got back to the laptop.

The job will be done as planned.

No, no, no.

She wrote, *It was a mistake. I want to cancel it.*

Typing…

A new message appeared. *No refunds, no cancellations.*

Florence stared at the screen. This was for real. A killer was actually going to murder Simon on her instructions. Then he'd demand another three thousand euro in bitcoin for doing it. And Florence would have to pay him.

You can keep the money, she wrote, her desperation hitting a new high. *Just forget about the job.*

Typing…

Then a new message.

It's not about the money. The job is guaranteed done within 24 hours. No refunds, no cancellations.

CHAPTER TWENTY-THREE

London, Friday, 9:55 am.

Thomas Ogden sat at the boarding gate in Heathrow. He wore a pale purple shirt and navy trousers. This, for him, was casual. He felt reasonably comfortable, but had been tempted to add a tie and jacket.

His briefcase contained false identification documents in a hidden compartment, but he wasn't using them for the flight. He thought that unnecessary. They were just a backup.

Brook Reynolds's death was all over the news. There was outrage from the tabloids. *LONDON GUN MURDER*. The zeitgeist would have flipped pretty quick if they'd known the real Brook Reynolds. It was a shame they'd never find out.

In the early hours of the morning he had developed his attack strategy and set the attack in motion. Florence's laptop was already compromised, but Thomas wanted to hack into her phone and Simon's phone too.

He'd established that their friend Ronan O'Brien was expecting them to visit him this evening in Claremorris. Ronan was friends with both Simon and Florence on Twitter. So Thomas had set up an account that looked exactly like Ronan's, and then sent Florence and Simon a message with a link in it. The link looked innocuous and, if they clicked on it, they'd see photos of the hotel they were meant to be staying in tonight.

What they wouldn't see was the malicious file that would run on their device, a trojan that gave Thomas control over their devices. So far, Simon had run the file. Thomas was confident that Florence would too. Thomas thought it was best to make sure he could track both of them. In this kind of situation, the more information you had, the better.

Young children ran around Thomas's feet, playing at being superheroes. He watched them fondly.

Thomas had his laptop open, so he noticed at once when a message came from the client. He read it with amusement. She was requesting cancellation of the job. Thomas took a sip of bland coffee and shook his head.

Compenso had never let anyone back out before, and they weren't going to start now. It wasn't about the money, although Thomas had already earmarked this client's fee to go towards his family holiday. More importantly, booking a hit showed the client's true intentions and those were the intentions which should be honoured. The cancellation request was nothing more than the death throes of a guilty conscience.

Thomas tapped out a quick reply.

The queue at the boarding gate was fifty or sixty deep. Thomas watched the family with the boisterous children as they joined the end of the line. Some people had already been standing in line for half an hour, looking stressed and bored. Meanwhile, Thomas sat a few feet away, perfectly comfortable, relaxing as he browsed on his laptop. He couldn't understand why they didn't sit down and take it easy until boarding began. They were going to end up in the same seats anyway.

Sometimes people don't know what was good for them. Sometimes an outside force had to apply pressure.

Thomas finished his coffee. He'd been up all night researching this job. He liked to know as much as he could about the people involved, and this job was a cinch.

Simon kept a low profile online, but he had an Instagram account. He liked to post pictures of the morning sun every day from the balcony of his apartment.

Thomas scrolled down impatiently, found some snaps from a trip to Portugal. One photo showed Simon and a blonde lady next to a river.

Thomas was pleased to see that Simon had tagged his girlfriend in that and many other pictures. Thomas clicked on her profile. Florence Lynch had nearly two thousand posts. All kinds of stuff. A gold mine. All of them with the locations tagged, friends tagged.

Simon Hill may not have documented much of his personal life, but his girlfriend's profile was full of photos of him and references to him.

An announcement crackled over the speaker.

"Attention please. Flight EI-415 is now boarding."

Thomas looked over, saw that the airline staff were still not letting people through. Dozens more passengers were now scampering to join the end of the queue.

Idiots.

Wendy would have been more charitable. She would have said they were cautious.

He kept scrolling through the Instagram feed. He found a picture of Florence and Simon together in Simon's apartment. They were both dressed up and grinning for the photo.

The line began moving.

Thomas waited until almost everyone had boarded, then packed up his laptop, took out his USB stick containing the TAILS operating system, and stuffed it into his jeans.

He walked over. There was no waiting. The airline staff checked his boarding pass and passport. A couple of seconds later, Thomas walked straight down the tunnel to the plane.

CHAPTER TWENTY-FOUR

Dublin, Friday, 10:31 am.
Stifling her panic, Florence scrolled through the rest of the previous day's chat with the hitman, cringing when she saw her own words on the screen. She had paid for the murder at 10:44 pm. So many hours had already passed. Simon would be dead before eleven o'clock tonight if the hitman was as good as his word.

Florence just wanted to crawl into her bed and die. But she needed to do something. She shifted her weight on the kitchen stool and stared at the laptop.

Think, Florence.

She ran her hands through her hair, trying to reassure herself. Her scalp itched beneath her fingers. All she could think was, *I'm screwed*.

Okay, she'd made a mistake, but there must be a way out, even if the hitman wouldn't cancel the job. All she had to do was stop him. But how? She didn't know who he was. And he probably knew how to mask his identity.

What else?

She couldn't bring in the authorities. Ending up in jail for twenty years as an accessory to murder wasn't how she planned to spend her forties and fifties.

She certainly couldn't tell Simon. He'd never forgive her. Worse, he'd insist on bringing in the authorities. Impossible. Florence could never let anyone find out what she'd done. Why should she? It was a mistake. Anyone could have made it. She'd been drunk, not in her right mind.

Daddy.

She'd have to ask her father to help. He'd know what to do, and he was the only one she trusted not to reveal her secret.

Florence felt a little better once she'd made the decision.

She went to the bathroom. For a moment she was appalled at the sight of her vomit all over the toilet and the floor tiles. It was impossible to face now. She decided she'd clean it up later. She stripped, dropping her clothes on the floor, switched on the shower and stepped under the warm water. Clumps of vomit were dried into her hair, so she had to wash it.

After the shower, she applied an aloe vera body cream to her legs and an expensive moisturiser to her face. She finished up with a few squirts of Chanel and selected her favourite outfit from the wardrobe. A black and grey dress with horizontal stripes, plus boots and a long beige coat. A thin red scarf gave her outfit a burst of colour.

Once dressed, Florence began to feel more confident. Like she could deal with this issue. She grabbed her keys and headed out the door.

Think of it as a business problem, she told herself as the elevator descended. Florence was a professional. What would she advise a client to do under these circumstances? A small business owner who accidentally got mixed up in murder?

Her phone rang, interrupting her thoughts. It was Hazel. Florence was inclined to believe Simon's explanation, to believe that nothing was going on between him and Hazel. Yet Florence wasn't sure, and she still felt a bubbling sense of distrust. She rejected the call as the elevator doors opened on the ground floor lobby.

Once outside her building, Florence set off walking to the tram, which was how she usually got to her office in Sandyford. Before she was banned from driving, she used to take her Lexus everywhere. Then she had one little accident and they took her license away. It was so unfair.

Fortunately, the tram took her almost to the door of her office. Her walk to the station in Ranelagh should have been pleasant. The June air was warm, the sky almost clear. Florence caught sight of bees buzzing around lavender flowers in the gardens she passed. She thought of Simon.

He had no idea his life was about to end.

Only three other commuters stood on the tram platform when she got there.

The sign said a southbound tram was due. It approached a moment later. The tram was much quieter now than it was during rush hour, when she normally rode it. For a change, Florence was able to get a seat. She crossed her legs and looked out the window.

Her head felt dreadful. Like her brain was bouncing around inside a dry, hollow skull. Closing her eyes didn't help. When she tried that, her head began to swim and she became dizzy.

She got her sunglasses out of her bag and slipped them on, then scrolled through Twitter, hoping it would distract her. There was a direct message from Ronan. He was boasting about how nice the hotel was, but to Florence it looked mediocre at best.

As the tram approached Sandyford, Florence's phone rang with another call from her father. She didn't answer. She'd be at the office soon enough, and she needed to explain things to him in person.

Would her father be able to believe that you could order a killer the same way you'd order a pizza? Well, she'd done it. And she could barely even remember how. She had a vague recollection of forums, e-mails, messages, exchanges, Tor and bitcoin.

As soon as the tram reached her stop, Florence stepped off. She set off walking briskly towards the office.

She ignored another call from her father. Nearly there. Lynch Business Success was located on the top floor of a three-storey office block.

The automatic doors opened as Florence arrived. She walked into the lobby.

Lynch Business Success read a small sign on the wall. It gave her pride every time she saw it.

She rode up in the elevator, stepping out at the top. The reception desk was just inside the door.

"Good morning," the receptionist said.

Her tone was flat, and her eyes lingered on Florence's shades. Florence straightened her back, held her head higher.

"Where's my father?" she asked.

"Here."

He stood at the end of the corridor. He looked as sharp as ever in his navy Louis Copeland suit, blue shirt and pale grey tie. But his expression was unusually dour.

"Hi Daddy."

"Follow me," he said. "You've got some explaining to do."

CHAPTER TWENTY-FIVE

Irish Airspace. Friday, 11:34 am.
Thomas Ogden gazed out the plane window as land appeared out of the Irish Sea. The distinctive bay and the two red and white chimneys rising high into the sky.

Dublin.

A city full of life and the good cheer. Thomas had visited the city a couple of times, once for a stag party in the Temple Bar area and once on a weekend break with Wendy. That was many years ago, before Freddy came along. Thomas remembered devouring oysters with stout, and taking a cruise around the bay. Fun times.

He'd never done a job here before.

Archie had a keen interest in Ireland. Amazingly enough, the man had his own Irish connections and they were pretty wild. Thomas had heard him rant about it that night in the Mayfair bar. The slave trade. Ethnic cleansing. The West Indies.

Thomas grinned.

His story really was wild.

Meanwhile Thomas had been ranting about Silk Road, the famous darknet marketplace. He'd told Archie about the clones that were popping up.

The next step had seemed obvious.

And they'd turned it into a reality.

Many would have thought that what Thomas was attempting today was impossible. Going to a city you didn't know and carrying out a flawless assassination within a matter of hours, then escaping the country the same day.

But the harder the task, the more satisfying it would be.

Thomas closed his laptop. He'd learned much. Simon Hill seemed like a bland, unassuming guy who'd never expect his girlfriend to have him murdered. The girlfriend herself seemed incredibly self-centered.

Thomas stroked his chin as he thought of her on the other end of a laptop tapping in the words, *I want him dead.*

Hard to imagine. Her online persona was so pleasant. Vacuous, but pleasant.

An announcement came over the speakers. The captain asked everyone to fasten their seatbelts, as they would be coming in to land shortly.

A flight attendant wheeled her cart of perfume away.

Tick tock.

The target would be dead in eleven hours at the latest.

CHAPTER TWENTY-SIX

Dublin, Friday, 11:45 am.

Florence followed her father down the corridor. She hated when he scolded her. Especially when it was in front of the staff. She wasn't a child, and she hated being spoken to as if she were. She stepped inside his office, and her father closed the door behind her.

"Don't sit down," he said.

He stood next to the desk and folded his arms.

"Is everything okay?" she asked.

From her perspective, nothing was okay, but she wondered why he was irate. Her father was normally so reasonable, so mild-mannered.

"What's the meaning of getting roaring drunk last night, coming in at midday, and ignoring my phone calls?"

"Oh, that—"

"Oh, that." He gave a humourless laugh. "Florence, you're a grown woman. Or you should be. You know, I think I was too soft on you when you were growing up. I shouldn't blame you. It isn't your fault you're spoilt. That's on me."

"What do you mean? I'm not spoilt."

He shook his head. A sad smile passed over his face.

"When your mother passed away, I tried to give you all the love I could. Enough for both of us. It looks like I didn't do a very good job. I should have helped you become independent."

"Daddy, I am independent. And you're the best. Please don't say such things."

Florence heard the ping of the lift down the corridor.

"That's probably my twelve o'clock," her father said.

He unfolded his arms and took a step towards the door.

Florence said, "Wait, I really need to talk to you."

There was no warmth in his eyes when he turned them on her. It shook her to see him like this.

"You've missed the whole morning, Florence. Go and do some work."

"This is important. It's life and death."

"Yeah. It always is with you."

"This is different. Seriously."

Her father sighed.

"I have a client waiting for me. You had two clients waiting for you and you never came, so I had to make excuses. You'll need to apologise to them. Now, please, leave me to my twelve o'clock and go wait for yours."

Did she have a meeting? Florence couldn't recall. Her brain wasn't working properly. And anyway she didn't care. She had more important things on her mind. There were only eleven hours left until Simon would be murdered on her instructions. Her father walked to the door. Before he went, Florence made one last try.

"Please, Daddy, I really need your help."

"Responsibility, Florence."

"What?"

"I made an appointment with a client. I have a responsibility to keep it."

He wasn't even listening to her.

"But *Daddy*—"

"Think about that word. Responsibility. I'm going now. We can talk at the end of the day." He opened the door, and paused before going out. "By the way, you made Jill cry. How do you feel about that?"

"What? Why?"

But he didn't answer. Just turned and walked away.

Florence couldn't quite believe it. His coldness. The way he'd left her to deal with this issue alone. What reason did Jill have to cry? If anyone had a right to feel upset, it was Florence. She was the one who'd suffered so much anguish. First, Simon may have cheated on her with Hazel, and now this business with the hitman was making her life absolute hell.

She left her father's office and headed down the corridor to her own. Jill was at her desk, outside Florence's office.

As usual, seeing Jill was a shock. Her PA was ghostly pale, with ink-black hair cut in a rigid fringe across her forehead, almost hiding her painted-on eyebrows. She wore a black blouse, and a long black skirt, with fishnet stockings and Doc Martins. The words *hello world* were tattooed onto the side of Jill's neck.

Florence wasn't sure she could handle the sight today. Jill could be useful when Florence had to use a spreadsheet or something, but she wished her assistant looked more presentable. And on the rare occasions when Simon had picked Florence up from the office, Jill had shown an unhealthy interest in him. Florence suspected that Jill had a crush. Not that it mattered, of course. Simon was way out of her league.

Florence cleared her throat.

"What's wrong with you, Jill?"

Her PA looked up. "Nothing, Florence."

"Good." An idea came to Florence. She said, "I have an urgent task for you."

"Okay." Jill grabbed a pen and notebook from the side of the table.

"I want you to find me a security guard who's available immediately."

Jill broke out in an amazed smile. "Wow. I had no idea we were getting a guard."

"Shushh," Florence said. "Keep your voice down. This is between you and me."

"Okay," Jill whispered. "Sorry."

"Call private security companies and draw up a shortlist of the best options and the cost."

Why hadn't Florence thought of it earlier? All she had to do was hire someone to protect Simon until 10:44 pm. If the job wasn't done by then, it would never be done. The hitman should give up on the contract once it was outside the 24-hour guarantee period.

"Do I have a meeting now?" Florence asked.

"Yes, with Jon Glynn."

"Jon Glynn? Who's that?"

"The IT guy?" Jill said. "With the trade mark problem?"

Another annoying habit of Jill's: turning everything into a question.

"Oh god. Is he here yet?"

"No," Jill said. "He called a moment ago to say he's running late. Something he had to deal with at the office?"

"Good."

Florence started to feel a little better. She'd solved the problem and was early for her meeting. She was tempted to ring her father and tell him, but maybe he wouldn't appreciate the interruption.

Anyway, it was fine.

Things had a way of working out. She only wished she wasn't so hungover.

"Find me a couple of painkillers. And I want that shortlist of security guards ready for me to check when my meeting is over. Actually, no, I want it ready in ten minutes."

"Okay."

Jill was still scribbling furiously as Florence went into her office. She opened the window so she could enjoy the warm June breeze on her face. Things were nearly sorted. Everything was going to be alright. She just knew it was.

CHAPTER TWENTY-SEVEN

Dublin, Friday, 11:55 am.
Once he'd gone through passport control, Thomas
Ogden headed straight to the toilets. The smell of
disinfectant filled the air. Biting and bitter, it made
his eyes water. Ducking inside a cubicle, he hung his
bag on the hook on the back of the door, and changed
clothes, swapping his sharp shirt for a black T-shirt,
and then adding a baseball cap.

Space was tight, but Thomas kept himself flexible
through daily exercise and copious stretching, and it
paid off at times like this. He had to keep in good
shape in his line of work. An unfit assassin was a
failed assassin, and Thomas had never failed at
anything.

He figured his plain navy trousers were fine and
he hadn't wanted to carry around a lot of clothes. The
baseball cap and T-shirt were minor changes but with
them Thomas looked quite different.

He still didn't know exactly how he'd deal with the target, but he wasn't worried. It's easy to kill a person. There are so many possibilities. And so many Thomas had not yet tried.

He stepped out of the cubicle and washed his hands at the sink. His eyes still burned from the chemical disinfectant. He took a bottle of eye drops from his bag and put a drop in each eye, then blinked rapidly to distribute the solution. Once his vision had cleared, he put on a pair of sunglasses. He slung his bag over his shoulder and left the toilets.

Ignoring the booming announcements over the PA, he walked towards the car rental booths. He started to remember this airport from his last trip. Sure, airports are pretty much the same. But they all have their quirks. Thomas recognised the bookshop, and the patisserie where he and Wendy had waited when their flight was delayed.

He looked forward to the holiday he'd promised Wendy. He wondered if it would be possible to do some work during it. The idea thrilled him.

He hired a car from Hertz and headed outside to collect the rental car. It was a five-year-old Nissan. Completely average and nondescript. Exactly what he needed.

Once he was behind the wheel, he stopped to check his phone. Both Simon and Florence had now downloaded the trojan file. The GPS on Simon's phone was turned off. With a few taps, Thomas turned it on. He wanted to make sure there'd be no surprises.

He set off in pursuit.

CHAPTER TWENTY-EIGHT

Dublin, Friday, 12:04 pm.
Florence's mood worsened when Jill brought her a cup of tea. Florence had stopped drinking tea the previous week and she'd specifically told her PA never to make tea again. She pushed the cup away from her.

"I don't want tea, Jill. I want coffee. Is that so hard to remember? Please bring me coffee and some painkillers. A decent coffee and lots of painkillers."

"Of course, Florence. Sorry."

Jill scurried away and came back a few minutes later with a cup of steaming coffee.

Florence popped two painkillers and drank the coffee, hoping the caffeine would help her perk up. As she waited for Jon Glynn, the twelve o'clock appointment, to arrive, her phone rang. Hazel again.

Florence stared at the screen a long time before answering. Finally, she pressed the green button and leaned back in her chair.

"What do you want?"

"Florence, what's going on? Simon said you acted crazy last night."

He has no idea, Florence thought.

She remembered Simon's text message, explaining that he'd been planning to propose to her. That he wasn't cheating. How Hazel had been helping him pick a suitable engagement ring. Florence wondered if it was true. Had Hazel really helped Simon pick out an engagement ring? Or was Florence's initial suspicion about an affair correct?

"Tell me the truth," Florence said. "How long has it been going on?"

"Oh my god," Hazel said. "I didn't believe Simon when he said you thought we're having an affair."

"I saw you in the street last night, so don't deny it."

"Saw what?"

"You and him kissing. Hazel, how could you?"

Hazel laughed. Did she think this was funny?

"Florence, we kissed because we were celebrating."

"Yeah. Celebrating your future together."

Hazel sighed loudly. "You probably need time to cool off. But I wanted to let you know that Simon plans to go to the jeweller's shop at lunchtime."

Florence sat straighter in her chair. "What are you talking about? What jeweller's shop?"

"Bartley's. He wants to get a refund on the engagement ring. I thought you might want to stop him. Of course, if you don't believe me and there's actually no engagement ring, then you don't need to do anything."

Florence held the phone tight in her hand. Her stomach twisted uncomfortably.

"I'm busy, Hazel. I don't have time for this nonsense."

She ended the call.

Still no sign of Jon Glynn. She was damned if she was going to wait here all day while the hours and minutes of Simon's life drained away.

She stepped outside her office.

"How's the shortlist coming along?"

"Good news," Jill boomed, flashing her perfectly even teeth.

Was she addressing everyone in the building? Florence looked around. Down the hall, a colleague poked his head above his desk divider to see what was going on.

"Keep your voice down," Florence hissed.

"Sorry," Jill said, in a voice that was not much quieter.

"What have you got?"

"I found one security company that can discuss our needs next week, and probably have a guard in the office at the start of next month. Would you like me to schedule a meeting with them?"

"That's utterly useless. Please use your head. I want a guard here in the next thirty minutes."

Jill's face slumped. "I didn't realise it was so urgent. That was the fastest one I've found so far."

"Keep looking." Florence reached inside her office door and pulled her coat off its hook on the wall. She adjusted her red scarf. "Call me when you find one."

"Are you going out?"

"Yes."

"What about Jon Glynn?"

Florence thought for a moment. "His office is in the city centre, isn't it?"

The north inner city, as she recalled. Close to Simon's office. That gave her a reason to be in the area. No one could accuse her of going to there just to check on Simon.

"Yes?" Jill said.

"Don't make everything a question."

"Sorry, Florence."

"Tell Jon Glynn I'll meet him at his own office instead of here. To make things easier for him."

She turned her back on Jill and headed for the elevator.

CHAPTER TWENTY-NINE

Dublin, Friday, 12:45 pm.
Simon had purchased the engagement ring in Bartley's, an upmarket shop with thick red carpet, mahogany-and-glass counters, and gleaming brass railings. The place smelled like furniture polish and looked like a gentleman's club. The prices matched that vibe. Hazel had talked Simon into splashing out big, and Simon had to agree because Florence wouldn't have listened to a proposal made with an inexpensive ring.

What an idiot I was, Simon thought.

He'd known Florence was selfish and fickle, yet somehow he'd convinced himself that she loved him, that she was even capable of love. He could see now how impossible that was.

He gripped the brass railing and stepped down a couple of carpeted steps to the main level of the shop, then headed to the counter. A tall man in his forties appeared behind it. The same staff member Simon had dealt with yesterday. Simon remembered that Will was his name.

Will had spent quite a while talking to Simon and Hazel yesterday, sizing up the pros and cons of the various options. A good salesman. By the time Simon paid, it felt like they were all old friends.

Like yesterday, Will wore a sharp suit, a gleaming watch and a shiny wedding ring. He had a handkerchief folded in his pocket and he gave off the smell of citrusy cologne. His longish hair was neatly parted in the middle, and swept back behind his ears. Careful presentation with a hint of boyishness.

"Good afternoon, sir," he said.

"Hi. Will, isn't it?"

"Indeed it is, sir. How are you today?"

Simon gave a weak smile. "Not as good as yesterday, I'm afraid."

Will frowned. "I'm sorry to hear that."

Simon felt in his pocket for the box. Still there, thank goodness. He pulled it out and set it down on the counter.

"I'd like to return this."

His face felt hot. How many losers did they see here, slinking sheepishly into the shop to return engagement rings?

Will opened the box. He looked at the ring inside.

"Was there a problem with this item?"

"No. I just… I don't need it."

Will nodded.

"Do you have your receipt?"

"Of course."

He found the piece of paper in his pocket and handed it over. Will looked at it and nodded.

"Would you like to exchange the ring for another item?"

"No, thanks. I'd like a refund."

Simon pulled his credit card from his wallet and held it out. Simon didn't like the way Will's frown deepened.

"I'm sorry, but we don't normally give refunds," Will said.

"Excuse me?"

"I'm happy to provide you with a credit note."

"That's no good to me. I don't buy fancy watches."

Will gave an apologetic smile. "On the plus side, it will have no expiry date."

"Oh great. The next time I think of proposing I can come back."

He squeezed his eyes shut.

Will said, "I'm very sorry. That's the best I can offer you."

"Fine," Simon said. He opened his eyes.

"You'll take a credit note?"

"What else can I do?"

He waited while Will processed the transaction. It seemed to take forever. Every second he stood there, Simon felt more humiliated. He could sense the other shoppers sneering at him. Still, Will tapped away at the computer. Was he writing an essay?

Finally, Will took out a small notepad and scrawled something on it. He tore off the sheet of paper and handed it to Simon. It was half the size of a postcard. The store's details were printed at the top of the page. The word *credit* and the amount were scrawled underneath, barely legible.

Simon picked up the paper, feeling how thin it was.

How flimsy.

He felt as if some kind of reverse alchemy had occurred. Yesterday, he'd come here with hopes and dreams and money. Now all that had been converted into a worthless quarter of a sheet of paper.

"You may like to look around?" Will said cautiously. "If not today, then on another occasion. As you'll appreciate, we have a wide selection. I'm sure I can help you find you something that would suit you. We have numerous gift options."

Simon turned away without a word. He walked to the door, and stepped outside in time to see Florence getting out of a taxi.

Florence looked awful. Dark circles hung under her bloodshot eyes. She saw him and hurried towards him across the footpath.

"What are you doing here?" Simon said. He felt suddenly weary.

"Hazel told me where you'd be."

"I don't want to see you."

"Well, I need to see you. I… Perhaps I made a mistake."

"Too late."

Simon tried to walk past her but Florence stepped in his path. "Simon, please wait. Listen to me. I've done something terrible."

"Add it to the list."

Florence's voice became petulant. "Just hang on for a second. Okay?"

"No," Simon snapped. He saw the shock on Florence's face. It brought him a grim feeling of satisfaction. She rarely heard that word.

"You owe me a chance to explain."

"I don't owe you anything," Simon said. He grabbed her hand and slapped the credit note down into it. "Here. You can buy yourself a candlestick or something. I don't want to see you ever again."

While she was still stunned into silence, he walked away.

CHAPTER THIRTY

Dublin, Friday, 1:15 pm.

Thomas watched the lovebirds from the other side of the street. An amusing demonstration. Simon Hill slapping a piece of paper into Florence Lynch's hand and storming off. The look of outrage on Ms. Lynch's face. Thomas had a feeling this moment wouldn't be documented on her Instagram feed.

Thomas had followed the target's phone from the airport, arriving only a couple of minutes ago. He'd stood opposite the shop and watched as Simon and Florence ran into one another. It was great timing, and Thomas was glad he got to see it.

Both Simon and Florence were easily recognisable from the photos Thomas had found, though Thomas felt he wasn't seeing them at their best today. Florence, in particular, looked dreadful, with her panda eyes and sunken cheeks. Thomas could catch all that from across the road. Up close, she must have looked even worse. Simon didn't look an awful lot better. His skin looked grey, as if he'd been drained of blood.

Thomas stared at them through his shades. He understood. The two of them had suffered a rough night. He'd pieced it together from Florence's confession, their text messages and Florence's voicemail. Thomas had access to all that. He knew what was going on. More or less.

Simon had cheated on Florence, then dumped her when she made a stink about it. Or, if you believed Simon, he'd been innocently buying an engagement ring, and had been accused groundlessly. Then he'd dumped her. Thomas didn't care which version was true. Probably neither of them.

Why were they even meeting? Thomas wondered about the jewellery shop. Was Simon returning the ring? They clearly hadn't reconciled, despite Florence's request to cancel the job. Her conscience was piping up a little too late. Or had a diamond ring changed her mind?

Anyway, cancel the job? Never. Thomas had told her the truth.

It *wasn't* about the money.

CHAPTER THIRTY-ONE

Dublin, Friday, 1:25 pm.
Florence stared at Simon's back as he walked away. His jacket billowed as he moved with his usual long stride, arms pumping, head low like an angry bull, his man-bun pointing towards the sun. The hair she'd run her fingers through so many times. When they'd started dating, she used to tease him about his love affair with hair gel. After a while, he stopped using it. But now, when it counted, Simon hadn't listened to her. She was trying to save his life and he was walking away.

A flash of rage blurred her vision.

That stupid fucking dope. How dare he walk out on her like this? Leaving her standing alone on the street?

A man bumped into Florence, knocking her out of her trance.

"Excuse me," she shouted.

Not that he cared. He didn't even look back.

The world was full of idiots.

She looked at the credit note. Her palm still stung from the force Simon used to slap it into her hand. The ring he'd bought had cost €4995. Did he really think that was an appropriate amount? Was that how much he loved her? Florence wouldn't have been able to hold her head up if she showed her friends such a cheap ring.

She squeezed her eyes shut.

Get a grip, Florence.

This was no time to get snotty. The credit note proved he'd intended to propose.

So he wasn't cheating on her.

She looked around the street. It was the usual lunchtime rush. People everywhere. The chatter of voices. The beeping of car horns.

Simon was going to have a bullet in his head in a few hours if she didn't do something. In fact, it could happen any second.

Would she be able to identify the assassin? What did they look like? She was pretty sure that he wasn't going to look like Keanu Reeves or any of those Hollywood hitmen.

Still not ready to face food, Florence's stomach turned when she caught the aroma of fish and chips on the air.

She took out her mobile and called Jill. As it rang, Florence thought about the situation. She'd arrange the security guard. However Simon felt about her, he needed to let a guard look after him for the rest of the day. She'd think of an excuse.

Two rings. Three.

What if Simon refused to accept protection? Florence decided she'd make the guard protect him anyway. He'd be safe whether he liked it or not.

"Florence?"

"Jill, you let the phone ring four times."

"I'm sorry."

"We can't afford to let it ring more than twice. It's really unprofessional. What if I was a client?" Florence stopped herself. She didn't have time for this. "What time will the security guard be ready?"

Jill cleared her throat.

"They can't start today."

"Then find someone else."

"I've called them all."

"Every security company in Dublin?"

"Yes, none of them can get someone to us today."

Jill probably *had* called every one of them. It would be just like her. Florence thought desperately but couldn't seem to get her brain into gear.

"And…"

Jill's voice was quiet.

"What is it?" Florence asked.

"Jon Glynn."

Florence had forgotten about him. She said, "I'm about to go there now." She thought she might as well, while she figured out what to do next.

"He said not to come."

"What?"

"He said forget it, that he doesn't want to work with us anymore."

"Bloody computer people."

Wait a minute.

Glynn was an IT whizz. So maybe he could help her. She'd hired not just a killer, but a killer on the darknet. A cybercriminal. Perhaps a hacker could get at him. What if Florence was able to unmask the hitman's identity? Then she might be able to stop him.

She couldn't turn him in without getting in trouble herself, but perhaps she could threaten him, force him to stop.

"Jill, I'm going to Glynn's office now."

"Like I said, he doesn't want to talk to us."

"I heard you. But I want to talk to him."

CHAPTER THIRTY-TWO

Dublin, Friday, 1:34 pm.

Simon stepped into the lobby of his building. Two colleagues were standing talking, one on his way out, the other on her way in. Simon ignored them and swiped through to the offices behind. He found Hazel at her desk, forking a tuna salad into her mouth.

"Why?" Simon called across the room. "Why did you do that?"

Hazel turned and looked at him, fork half-raised to her mouth.

"Huh?"

"Don't huh me."

Simon made his way over and stopped right next to her.

"Okay, okay," Hazel said. "I told Florence you were going to return the ring. Did it not go well? I just wanted to let her know."

"I already let *you* know that I was finished with her. I told you that. I haven't changed my mind."

He felt so angry he could hardly speak. And beneath that, there was a sad ache. Seeing Florence had been painful. Hazel seemed to read his expression. She touched his arm.

"Sit down, Simon. I'm sorry."

He dropped into the chair next to her.

"If you don't want to go to the party, you don't have to."

Simon's eyes were suddenly itchy. He rubbed them until they watered. That made them worse, but he forced himself to stop.

Hazel was leaning forward in her chair, the salad forgotten.

"I said I'd go," Simon said. "So I'll go. That's how I am."

"Okay."

"I mean what I say."

"Alright. Shit. I'm sorry. I just thought I should let her know. In case she could make it up to you somehow." Hazel shrugged.

"Forget it," Simon said with a sigh.

After a moment, Hazel smiled. "Tonight will be fun. We haven't seen Ronan in so long."

"Everyone will be drinking," Simon said miserably.

"I have your back. If I see a drop of booze in your hand, I'll punish you."

Maybe the birthday bash would take his mind off Florence. A night away from home might help. And when he returned home the next day he'd … what? Download a dating app?

"What am I going to do?" Simon said miserably.

Hazel took his chin between her fingers and tilted it up.

"Tonight, we're going to have fun," she said. "That's all you need to think about."

CHAPTER THIRTY-THREE

Dublin, Friday, 1:45 pm.
Jon Glynn's company had offices in a tall Georgian townhouse not far from Bartley's jewellery shop. Florence had always been interested in these buildings. They had been constructed to house a single wealthy family and their servants. Around the turn of the twentieth century, many of them had been converted into multi-family homes. Slums, housing maybe a hundred people.

It gave Florence the creeps. She thought of all those people. They had no personal space. No plumbing.

It was even worse than a jail cell.

Florence shuddered, though the air was mild. No, she wasn't going to jail. No one was going to kill Simon. She'd make sure of that.

A homeless man sat on the steps outside the building. Weeds sprouted through cracks in the footpath at his feet. He glanced up at Florence. He shook his head, got to his feet and staggered down the road.

It was as if he had looked into her soul, and seen... nothing. A hole where her heart should have been.

She shook her hair and plunged her hand into the pocket of her coat. Her fingers grazed the credit note. Simon really had intended to propose in the ramen bar, over noodles. Hazel really had helped Simon pick it out.

It was true that he would have needed guidance, though Florence wouldn't have chosen Hazel. Hazel knew the kind of stuff Florence liked, but her own style was a little uncouth. Always had been. Florence remembered the chunky earrings Hazel used to wear in school. She remembered joking that Hazel could use them as weights if she took up bodybuilding.

Cruel but true.

Florence fortified herself with a squirt of Chanel, then hurried up the steps. Her laptop bag was swung over her shoulder. She liked to keep it with her, despite its weight. She pressed the buzzer and the door unlocked.

Inside was a tiled lobby. There was no one around, but a directory on the wall listed the companies on the different floors. Glynn Enterprises was on three.

Florence's boots made a racket as she walked across the floor. There was no elevator so she hurried up the stairs. The steps were lined with a threadbare runner. On the second-floor landing, she heard a screaming match from behind a closed door.

What a place, Florence thought, adjusting her scarf nervously.

No wonder Jon Glynn had asked so many questions about her fees upfront. Money must be tight if he was renting workspace in this kip. There were a couple of doors on the third-floor landing. Poky little offices. A plaque reading *Glynn Enterprises* was stuck on the wall next to a door.

She knocked and went in without waiting.

Florence found herself in the middle of a tiny office. She was almost on top of the desk nearest the door. A woman with huge glasses sat behind it. Another desk lay on the other side of the room. A badgered looking man sat behind it talking on the phone. The doorway to a private office lay beyond that.

The place reminded Florence of a caravan. A tiny little caravan. Everything was so tight.

"Can I help you?" the woman asked.

Florence ignored her and made for the closed door. It had to belong to Glynn. She marched in. Sure enough, Jon Glynn sat behind the desk. He was a big man in his forties, with hardly any hair left, and a gut that pressed against his shirt and hung down over his belt. He looked up when she entered the room.

"Ms. Lynch? I told your secretary—" Jon Glynn said.

Florence slammed the door behind her.

"I know. I apologise." She sank into the chair opposite him before he could kick her out. Glynn looked a little shamefaced. Florence watched his eyes as they flitted around the room, as if to remind himself of his position. He'd been in her glossy office and now she was seeing how modest his was.

There were computer components, tablets and laptops piled up on one side of the room. The room smelled faintly of damp. Florence could imagine spores snaking their way into her lungs.

Better make this quick.

"I need your help," she said.

Glynn gave a snort of laughter. "I think I'm the one paying *you* for advice. At least, I was."

"I know, but something came up. I'm being targeted by a hacker."

"I thought we were meant to be having a meeting about my business."

"We will," Florence snapped. "But can you help me?"

"What kind of attack?"

"It's—"

Glynn waved his hands. "Actually, never mind. I don't care. I care about my trade mark. I care about getting this business off the ground and getting more clients. But you're pre-occupied with your own affairs."

"Jon, it's not like that," Florence said, using her most soothing voice.

"I told your assistant I'm done with your company. I've never seen such an unprofessional people in my life."

Florence stifled a sharp retort. Without a security guard, Glynn was her only hope at saving Simon. She couldn't afford to mess this up.

"I'll pay you," she said.

Glynn snorted. "I wouldn't count on it. You'd probably change your mind about that, the same way you changed your mind about today's meeting."

"You're the one who was late," Florence snapped. "The answer is still no."

"I need you. Tell me, why were you delayed?"

Glynn leaned back in his chair and sighed.

"If you must know, I ordered a spare part for one of my machines. A very expensive piece."

"So what's wrong? Did it arrive broken?"

Glynn shook his head. "It arrived fine. But then a second one arrived. They've charged me for two, but I only wanted one."

Florence nodded. She'd been hoping it would be something she could help him with, but there was nothing she could work with there.

"What about your trade mark problem?"

"It doesn't matter."

"I help you and you help me, okay?" She saw the papers on his desk. Recognised the logo of the Intellectual Property Office of Ireland. Before he could stop her, she grabbed the letter and pulled it towards her.

"Hey, that's private."

Florence scanned it quickly.

"It's only an objection. We can overcome it." She pulled his laptop towards her, but Glynn pulled it back at once.

"Ms. Lynch?"

"Yes?"

"You're fired. Fired. I can spell the word for you if you like. Get out of my office."

"This is the gratitude I get?" Florence stood up. Her chest swelled with indignation. She'd kicked a few people out of her office in her time – usually Jill – but never had Florence been on the receiving end.

She said, "Fine. I hope your grubby little business dies."

"That's lovely."

Florence turned on her heel and walked out the door.

Head high, back straight. All the way until she got to the stairs again. At that point she leaned against the wall and wondered what the hell she could do now.

She took a moment to compose herself, then made her way down the stairs, out onto the street. Along the way, an idea burst into her mind. Glynn's problem with his component had inspired her.

It only took a minute to find a café down the road. The place was busy because of lunch hour but Florence found a table in the corner and got out her laptop.

She needed to talk to the people at Compenso again.

CHAPTER THIRTY-FOUR

London, Friday, 2:03 pm.
Few defendants appearing before Archie Browne did not do a double-take when they saw a dark-skinned man with bright red hair presiding over their trial. They looked at him even harder when they realised it was his natural hair colour and that his eyes were an icy blue. Archie missed those days.

He was at home, standing in the kitchen of the house he shared with his wife in Bexley, when his phone beeped. He was washing up after lunch. Lucinda, his wife of thirty-three years, was drying. She shot him a look.

"You *are* active at the moment with your retirement projects."

"I am," Archie agreed in a deep baritone. Giving Lucinda the wolfish grin he knew she still loved, he dried his hands on a towel.

"What is it now?" she asked.

"I'm not a mind-reader, woman. Let's see."

"Don't forget the fundraiser is tonight."

As if Archie was going to forget that. The event was a work of passion. "I'm the one who's responsible for it."

"That you are," Lucinda said.

"Someone should organise a fundraiser for me," he added. It was a joke. However, since the Queen had seen fit to remove him from the Crown Court, Archie had certainly felt the pinch. You missed two hundred thousand pounds a year. The humiliation was more painful than the financial loss. And though he lived modestly, by the standards of his ancestors he was rich beyond belief.

In any case, he'd kept himself busy since being removed from the judiciary.

Archie still longed to see things set right. But sometimes justice needed a helping hand.

That was what tonight's fundraiser was about. Raising money to investigate possible mishandling of cases in the justice system. It had been arranged a long time ago, while he was still a judge, and he knew that these days he would not be welcome at the event. One of the other organisers had discreetly tried to dissuade him from attending. Said Archie would taint it, make them all look like extremists. Well, tough.

Then there was his other work, where he was not Archie Browne, disgraced Crown Court judge, but Imperator, a faceless phantom, a crackle of zeros and ones.

He puttered into the study where he'd left his phone, his slippers moving noiselessly on the bare wood floor. He was wearing his new trousers, the ones with a wider waistline, and thank goodness for that. Lunch demanded some room for expansion. As he reached his mid-sixties, Archie found everything a little harder than it used to be.

More aches and pains, but that was nothing compared to the appalling disease and squalor his ancestors had endured.

Three framed maps hung over his desk. One of Barbados, one of Ireland, and one of the United Kingdom. Often, when he came into the room, he paused to reflect on the three places that had formed his identity.

In the 1650s, the British had branded the forefather he was named after, the original Archie Browne, a troublemaker. He had been taken forcibly from Ireland and shipped to Barbados. *Indentured servant* was the euphemism, but Archie preferred the word *slave*. He was one of the Red Legs, the poor white underclass formed by these relocated labourers. Maybe the name came from their trouble handling the Caribbean sun. Archie wasn't sure. In any case, his ancestor had been promised his own land once he completed twenty years' work on a sugar plantation. Of course he'd died in squalor before the twenty years was up. And even if he hadn't, there was no land to give him. Barbados is only 169 square miles. The promised land had never existed. Before he died, he'd married a local woman, and the line continued, all the way down to Archie and his children.

Most Red Legs lived in dire poverty, even the small number still alive now. But Archie had been lucky. In 1948, his father had saved the life of a visiting Englishman, when he was attacked by some locals in Bridgetown. That man had been a civil servant in the British government. To show his gratitude, he'd helped Archie's father relocate to England, where Archie was born.

So British hands had exiled his kin to Barbados and British hands had helped bring him to London. Archie didn't hate the British. There was no sense in hating a whole people just because some of them treated him bad. Some of them treated him good too. Hell, Lucinda was an English rose if ever he'd seen one. A milky-skinned beauty from Somerset who traced her genealogy back six hundred years.

Archie had been born in London, but he felt like he'd spent his whole life fighting to be English. A scholarship to Cambridge had helped. Classics at university, then law. A career in the magistrates' court and then the Crown Court, distinguished by sentences that some said were harsh, and pronouncements that some said had no place in a judge's mouth. And then it had all been taken away from him at the age of 62.

Now he did what needed to be done.

He balanced.

Compenso.

He looked at his phone and ran a hand through his greying curls as he read the message.

"Oh my."

From the next room, his wife called, "What is it, Archie?"

"Nothing."

He trusted Lucinda with his life, but he didn't trust her with his secrets.

Archie shook his head in admiration. The client had stopped looking for a rcfund. Now she had a new idea.

Will you people target anyone at all? I purchased the services of one of your operatives last night. I want to hire another one now. I want them to kill the first guy before he does the job.

Archie gazed at the slapdash phrasing, considered the murderous intent, and shook his head in mute admiration. He needed to go upstairs and find the encrypted phone he used to communicate with his Irish operative.

CHAPTER THIRTY-FIVE

Dublin. Friday, 2:25 pm.

Kim Roberts was sunning herself in the back garden when her phone pinged. Her second phone. She hadn't heard it make that noise for seven months. The last time she heard it, someone died hours later.

Kim sat up in her deck chair. The fabric beneath her groaned at the movement of her naked body. Maybe she'd put on a few pounds since she quit her job at the auto repair shop. Okay, a few dozen pounds. But it didn't matter anymore. Not since Dr. O'Neill's diagnosis stuck a pin in her balloon.

"Mmmmmm."

The sound came from the back of Kim's throat. It was like a dog growling. Her cat, Napoleon, was walking along the garden fence to her right. He froze and stared at Kim. He hated it when she made that noise.

"Something's up, Bony."

Imperator. The mysterious mastermind behind Compenso. That was who the message was from. Kim hadn't stopped thinking about the last job she did for the organisation. And she'd kept the encrypted phone to hand in case her assistance was required again.

She scraped back her curly grey hair, felt it tickle her shoulders. When she'd worked as a mechanic, she'd worn her hair in a severe ponytail. These days she normally let it hang loose.

She let everything hang loose.

And, wow, did that feel good.

Kim had always wanted to be a soldier. Ever since she was a little girl. Now, in her final days, she regretted missing out on that experience. Of course, she shouldn't have headbutted that Defence Forces recruitment officer. But *he* shouldn't have called her fat.

She felt around under her ass for her stringy bikini. Funny, she'd always been so shy. Only since retirement had she started to get out of her comfort zone. She thought of it as retirement, but it wasn't really. She'd quit her job at the auto shop after Dr. O'Neill said the tumour in her brain would kill her by Christmas. There just didn't seem much point fixing cars when she was falling apart herself. And the weeks of chemo she tried did nothing but make her feel like hell, and age her a decade. She was 53 but could easily pass for 65 now. The last time she'd been on a bus, some little shit had seen her standing and offered her his seat.

She swung her legs over the side of the chair, making it groan again. She was afraid she was going to break the chair one of these days. That was why she positioned it on the grass instead of on the patio. She'd have a softer landing if her ass ever punched through the worn old fabric.

Napoleon watched as Kim stood up and stretched her big arms and legs. The damn cat always looked so judgmental. She'd meant to take up tai chi when she stopped working, maybe yoga too, but that had never happened. Happy hour started coming earlier. That was all that had happened.

Especially on June days like this – sunny, blue sky, twenty-three degrees Celsius – Kim liked nothing more than to sit in the garden and listen to the birds sing.

She stepped into her pink bikini bottoms. Then she found the top, and slipped it on. Her neighbours could have been watching from their bedroom windows. There were houses on each side of her and also behind.

But Kim really didn't give a damn anymore. Decades of being uptight about her body and what had it got her?

"Diddly squat," she told Napoleon.

Kim was surprised to see that her legs and belly were almost as pink as the bikini. She wiped the sweat off her upper lip.

"I look like a piece of bacon," she muttered.

Napoleon mewed as if he agreed.

She'd spent too long under the sun. She could feel the prickle on her skin. Later it would be sore. That was for sure. She found her flip flops and walked across the garden to the table where both her phones sat.

Call me ASAP, Imperator's message read.

She stepped into the house to make sure none of her neighbours were able to overhear the conversation. This house wasn't hers. She shared it with four other tenants, but no one else was home at the moment.

In the kitchen, she opened the fridge and pressed her ass against the shelves, almost sitting inside it. She would have done that if she was able to fit. The coldness felt fantastic on her back.

In that position, she rang Imperator. The call was answered after one ring.

"Fiat justitia…" a distorted voice said. It was just as unnerving as it had been last time. Kim had no idea if she was talking to a man or a woman, if they were young or old. She knew Imperator was based in the U.K., but that was about all. She'd "met" Imperator online, on a true crime message board, and their worldview seemed amazingly similar.

"… ruat caelum," Kim replied, completing the Latin sentence. "This is a surprise."

"We have a job in Ireland."

"I'm listening."

"You don't need to do it."

"I'm listening," Kim said again. She waited to hear the details. Who would it be this time? And how much would Kim be paid?

Imperator's distorted voiced boomed out of the phone. "This one is… unusual. The client has already hired an operative to kill her boyfriend."

Nothing hurt like love. Kim was glad she'd never really got serious about anyone. It would be hell now if she had. As it was, she had no one to say goodbye to except her mother and her brother, though he was in prison and she wasn't sure she wanted to go there anymore.

"Why do you need me?" Kim asked.

"The client changed her mind."

"Ha."

"You know our policy on cancellations."

"No cancellations. No refunds."

She was quoting what she had been told at the start. A distorted laugh from the other end of the line.

"Right. No backing out."

Kim said, "So?"

"The first operative has been deployed from London."

"Why wasn't I called about this earlier? You sent someone from London?"

"The first unit asked for this job."

"Okay," Kim said slowly. Maybe the other operative was desperate for the money? Kim waited for more information.

"The client wants to target that operative."

Kim rubbed her eyes. "This woman wants us to kill one of our own people."

"You got it. To prevent that operative from completing the job."

"Amazing. Has this ever happened before?"

"No," Imperator said. "Never."

Kim's backside was getting cold now. She turned around so that the cool air washed over her chest and belly. Damn, that felt good. She opened the ice box too, to make the effect stronger.

Imperator said, "I'm concerned about this operative. His recklessness. I want you make sure he doesn't cock it up."

"You don't want me to do the job? To kill him?"

"Of course not."

Kim said, "I guess our man is closing in."

"He is."

"How do you know it won't all be over before I get out of the house?"

"I am keeping an eye on him. I can feed you information he procured about the target. That will help you catch up."

"You can do that? You're monitoring him?"

A long pause.

Then Imperator said, "I was worried. He seems to be enjoying the work a little too much. He is eager for another job. And another job. And another."

"So you hacked him? How?"

"I'd rather not get into the details. Suffice it to say, I *am* watching him."

"Are you spying on me too?"

"Don't be ridiculous," Imperator said. "So, are you in or out?"

Didn't actually answer the question, Kim noted. She gazed out the window, wondering if a drone was hovering overhead. Was her laptop compromised? Her phone?

Truth was, she didn't give a shit. Most of the time, she was bored and sluggish and sad.

Kim said, "I'm in."

"Good. I'll set it up for you. Forward you what you need to know. You'll need to move fast."

"I'll get ready," Kim said.

The line went dead.

Kim stepped back from the fridge and closed its door.

"Mmmmmm," Kim growled. She caught sight of Napoleon standing at the door to the garden, an unhappy look in his eyes. "Time to get to work, Bony," she said.

CHAPTER THIRTY-SIX

Dublin, Friday, 2:48 pm.

As soon as the bitcoin transfer was complete, Florence slammed her laptop shut. Second time was easier. Memories of the previous night came back to her, and she had forgotten that Compenso provided her with a document full of instructions. She broke out in such a demented grin that the guy at the next table stopped checking her out, and actually moved his chair away.

This computer stuff was meant to be fast, but Florence felt like she'd been sitting in the café forever. The waiter had been pressuring her to order food or else leave, ever since she finished her espresso. Her compromise had been to order a second espresso, as she was still uncertain if her stomach could handle food.

Florence didn't know why she hadn't thought of the solution earlier, when it was so obvious. Why get a security guard to protect Simon from the hitman she'd hired, when she could just hire a second hitman to kill the first one?

It was perfect. They were cold-blooded killers. It wasn't like they cared who they hurt.

Compenso had no qualms about taking the assignment. The organisation's price was triple, though, because of the urgency, and to compensate for the cost of losing an operative.

Can it be done? Florence had asked. *Is there enough time?*

She was conscious of the 24-hour guarantee. Hours, minutes and seconds ticking by. Then the reply came.

We'll put our best operative on it.

Please hurry! How will I know when you got the job done?

We'll make sure you know.

Perfect. thanks xxx

Three kisses. Shit. That was how Florence signed almost every text, e-mail, and Instagram post. And she'd included it in her encrypted message to a gang of murderers without even noticing.

She had a fleeing moment in which the world seemed to bend into surreal shapes. Her fingers gripped the armrest of her chair as if it was a life raft.

Her perfect life had gone to hell in a matter of hours. How was that possible? A good job, a perfect partner, a great friend, the best father she could have asked for – everything in her life was falling apart.

She tried to shake the feeling off. Simon was safe. Or he soon would be. That was what mattered. She wasn't worried about the relationship. They could patch that up later.

As she stepped out of the café, into the afternoon sun, her phone rang. It was her father. She didn't quite feel up to speaking with him, so held off answering even though she knew he'd be mad.

With her head back, she strode down the street. She decided to try talking to Simon. To tell him that, for his own safety, he needed to go straight home after work. Luckily, that was his usual routine. Unlike her, he was a bit of a homebody.

Simon's office came into view ahead. Florence only hoped he'd speak to her.

She entered the lobby and approached reception as the elevator next to the desk pinged. Simon and Hazel stepped out, bags slung over their shoulders.

What were they doing?

In a flash, Florence remembered Ronan's party. Florence was meant to be going too. With everything going on, she'd forgotten. Of course, she wasn't going. Not while her relationship with Simon was in such turmoil. She wouldn't have expected Simon to go either.

But here he was with an overnight bag – one Florence had bought him, actually – and a blank look on his face.

Hazel looked shocked to see Florence, but Simon didn't even slow his pace.

"Simon? I need to talk to you."

He held up a hand. "I've said everything I want to say to you."

"But… you're not still going to Ronan's party, are you?"

She grabbed his arm. With a sigh, Simon turned to her.

"Why not? He's *my* friend."

Florence turned to Hazel, who shrugged.

"I'm just following the plan," she said.

"But you broke up with Harry, didn't you?"

"Gary," Hazel said. "So what? I'm still going to my friend's birthday party. Who cares if I don't have a date?"

"But—"

"Simon can keep me company."

Florence didn't like this. She wanted to keep an eye on Simon. She couldn't have him driving across the country to a strange hotel, a place full of strangers.

Or would it be safer there? The hitman would be coming here, to the office, or more likely going to Simon's home later in the evening. Florence had a flashback to last night, when she'd asked about the professional way to kill a person. The answer had been, *two bullets in the back of the head when they arrive home.*

So the trip might actually be a good idea. Still, Florence didn't feel right watching Simon and Hazel go off together like this.

And was there a hint of mischief in Hazel's eye? An infuriatingly superior look? No. Surely not. Hazel had given her a heads-up about the jewellery shop. It was just a pity Florence hadn't got there sooner. Then she might have a ring on her finger instead of a credit note in her pocket.

"I still want to go," Florence said.

"You can't," Simon said. "You're not invited."

"Of course I am. I was planning to go."

Simon shook his head. "Ronan invited me. You were to be my plus one. Now I don't want you as my guest, so you're not welcome."

If her hangover hadn't dulled her reaction time, Florence's jaw might have hit the floor in the time it took Simon and Hazel to breeze past her.

You're not welcome.

When had Simon turned so cold? All she'd done was throw one stupid tantrum, and this was the result?

She hurried to the door. Simon and Hazel were already across the street. They threw their overnight bags on the backseat of Hazel's car, then got in.

Blood pounded in Florence's head as they car moved away. She could hear it. She could feel it.

She couldn't just wait for Simon to see if Simon came back alive the next day.

She got on her phone and called Jill.

"It's me," she said. "I need you to pick me up. And bring a toothbrush. I hope you don't have plans for tonight."

CHAPTER THIRTY-SEVEN

Dublin, Friday, 2:50 pm.
Kim Roberts slung her handbag over her shoulder and went out the door, leaving Napoleon in the house.

Kim thought, *By the time I return home, someone will be dead.*

One of her housemates would take care of the cat if anything happened to her.

"Wish me luck, Bony," she whispered.

The cat watched her scornfully as she made her way down the driveway.

She walked to her mother's house, which was ten minutes away, in Terenure. Vera Roberts was seventy-two. She'd lived alone since the death of her husband. Kim knocked on the door and waited. She had a key, but her mother hated it when Kim burst in unannounced.

"I might be with a gentleman friend," Vera would say whenever the topic came up.

And the creepy thing was, she might. She was part of an active retirement community that met every week at the local library. Teenage hormones were long gone, but as far as Kim could tell, these OAPs spent half their time flirting.

Kim was about to knock a second time when Vera opened the door. She had girlish clips in her hair and wore a cardigan Kim hadn't seen before.

"Looking good, mum."

Vera smiled. "I ordered a few outfits online. They came this morning."

Kim held her tongue. Her mother had learned to love online shopping thanks to the active retirement group. She'd never been interested in the internet when Kim tried to teach her about it.

"Am I interrupting?" Kim said.

"No, but Tommy from the club is coming over in an hour."

"I'll be gone by then. I just wanted to drop in and say hi."

Vera stepped back. "Come in, come in. I'll make tea."

"Not sure I have time for that."

Kim stepped inside. The house was warm and she could smell baking. Soda bread, fresh from the oven. What a smell. Kim didn't know she was hungry until she caught that aroma. So many memories came with it. Vera made the same bread today that she had in 1960.

"Of course you have time." Vera smiled. "In case you forgot, you're retired now, just like me."

Kim nodded slowly. She hadn't told her about the tumour. As far as Vera was concerned, Kim had taken early retirement because the auto-shop wanted to reduce its costs.

"How *is* retirement?" Vera asked.

"Heaven."

Kim didn't want her mother to know how hard she was finding it since she stopped working. Her days had no routine and she stayed up later each night. These days, she often went to bed at 3 am, and it was lunchtime when she got up. Standards were slipping and she felt a dreadful aimlessness. She had nothing to do but wait to die.

Unlike her mother, Kim had no gentleman callers. She only had Napoleon for company and that damn cat gave every indication that he despised her.

The only thing that excited her was her clandestine activity for Compenso. That was a thrill that took her out of her dull existence.

And it was something she felt proud of.

Vera set off for the kitchen. "I'll put the kettle on," she said.

"I'm going to use the loo, mum."

Kim went to the staircase.

"I don't know why you never use the one downstairs," Vera said.

The house had two floors and Vera rarely went upstairs anymore. The steps were hard on her knees. And everything she needed was on the ground floor. The old dining room had been converted into her bedroom years ago. It had a roomy en suite with hand rails on the walls and in the shower stall. Kim would have liked to move back here, but then her mother would see her fade away.

"You know I prefer the other bathroom," Kim said. "Always have."

Kim had grown up in this house. She liked to come up here and wander around all the rooms once in a while.

At the top of the stairs, she turned away from the bathroom and headed to her brother, Phil's old bedroom. It was basically a junk room now. Cardboard boxes, piles of vacuum-packed clothes, stuffed bookshelves. There was hardly space to get into the room. Cobwebs had been built between islands of junk.

Kim walked to the window, her shoes making noise on the old wooden floor. Her knees cracked when she hunkered down.

"Jesus!" she gasped.

"What are you doing?" Lucinda called. "I thought you wanted to use the loo."

"Give me a second, mum."

Like Kim, Phil had always wanted to be a soldier, but unlike her he'd actually joined the Defence Forces.

Kim lifted the loose floorboard. The gun lay where Phil had left it. It was a semi-automatic pistol, a Heckler & Koch USP. She'd brought it with her on the last job too, though she hadn't used it. There was no reason she'd need to use it today, either, if Compenso was being upfront with her. After all, she was just meant to observe her colleague.

A spider scuttled across the barrel of the gun. Kim got a tissue from her pocket and wiped it, then lifted it up and admired it.

During his time in the Defence Forces, her brother had built a lucrative side-line sneaking arms out of the barracks and selling them on the black market. Guns, explosives. You name it. He would have stolen the tanks if he could. No one was surprised when Phil was discharged. But it wasn't for stealing weapons. It was for pointing a gun at a senior officer. He wasn't a bad man, really. Just couldn't control himself.

Kim retrieved a grenade from under the floorboards too. The Defence Forces favoured the Mecar M72, a Belgian-made fragmentation grenade. Four seconds after pulling the pin, the detonation sent 900 shards of fragmentation and dozens of ball bearings shooting through the air.

Kim had never used a grenade. But she'd always wanted to, at least once before she died.

Maybe she should go and see Phil while she still had time. He was serving a sentence for manslaughter in Mountjoy Prison. Kim hadn't visited him for a while. It was so sad to see him in there.

All he'd done was stop their father beating Vera one night. But he used a little too much force. Their father was gone, and Phil's life was ruined. Was that justice? He'd only been protecting Kim and Vera.

Kim sighed, put the gun and grenade in her bag, replaced the loose floorboard, and went to the bathroom. Just to satisfy her mother.

She got the glass that held a spare toothbrush, filled it with water and poured the water into the bowl, then flushed the toilet.

She eased downstairs, mindful of her own creaking joints.

Her mother was sitting at the kitchen table with a teapot in the middle of the table. Next to it, a plate was piled high with iced buns.

"Have a bun. Have a cup of tea. Though it will probably set you off again. You piss like a racehorse, Kim."

"Thanks, mum."

They both burst out laughing.

"Arthur Miller's mother said that about—"

"Marilyn Monroe. You told me the story, mum."

"Because she ran the tap so no one would hear her pee."

Kim nodded. "I know, mum."

They ate the buns, still hot, and slathered in melting butter. Kim needed fortification before she faced the job ahead.

CHAPTER THIRTY-EIGHT

Kildare, Friday, 3:21 pm.

With her hands resting on the steering wheel, Hazel glanced at Simon. They had left Dublin behind and he still hadn't said a word. Now they were speeding down the motorway. There wasn't much to see on either side of the road. Just glimpses of cows in fields.

Hazel's window had been open a little, but the smell of cow dung and hay now filled the air. She closed the window.

Simon stared out the passenger window, a morose expression on his face.

Hazel said, "Will you really not give Florence a chance?"

"Never," Simon said.

He sounded irritated that she'd asked again. Hazel hadn't seen him so adamant about anything for as long as she had known him. Honestly, she'd thought he might crack when Florence appeared at the office. But he hcld firm. Good for him.

When a couple broke up, you had to pick one to stick with. So who would Hazel choose? Florence, her infuriating best friend since she was thirteen, or Simon, her heartbroken colleague?

It should have been an easy choice. Friends stick together. But the truth was, Florence was insufferable sometimes.

Hazel punched Simon on the arm.

"Ow. What was that for?"

"Don't look so miserable. Buck up and tell me what you got Ronan. It better be something good. I mean, he's turning fifty. You need a decent gift for someone's fiftieth."

Simon sat straighter in his seat and rubbed his arm.

"Yeah, well. I got him a gift voucher."

"Nice. Love the personal touch."

Simon scowled. "What did you get him?"

Hazel smiled. "A very nice jacket."

"Wow."

Simon's voice dripped with sarcasm.

Hazel kept driving. Another two hours. Then some food and the birthday bash. Then a night in a fancy hotel.

"Did you know that Florence once stole my boyfriend?"

Simon perked up. "What? When?"

"I was fifteen and madly in love with a guy named Colm Quinn who was on the school basketball team. He was a big, tall guy. After wanting to go out with him for about two years, I finally asked him to go to McDonald's with me."

"On a date?"

"I guess. I told him he was my boyfriend. He didn't contradict me."

Simon laughed. "I bet he didn't. He was probably scared. So you had a whirlwind romance?"

"Yes, if you mean that he started walking me home from school."

"What did Florence do?"

"One day he didn't walk me home. I didn't know where he was. I waited for him outside school for ages. Finally, I gave up and started walking home. I found him kissing Florence in the field near my house. Actually, Florence was kissing him. I… I don't know, but I felt like she was doing it just to spite me. Just to show she could. She was so pretty, even then. It's childish, but I was devastated. Cried myself to sleep for a month."

"That's awful. Were they together long?"

"She lost interest in him after a week."

Simon shook his head. "I'm sorry."

"Don't be silly," Hazel said. "I'm sorry. I set you up with her."

"We had some good times together."

"I'm not saying she's a bad person," Hazel said. "I mean, despite Colm Quinn, we turned out to be good friends. But… you know Florence."

"Right," Simon said. "I know Florence."

CHAPTER THIRTY-NINE

Dublin, Friday, 3:25 pm.

Florence waited outside Simon's building. She kept looking around in case anyone suspicious was lurking nearby. *The killer.* She saw no one weird. Just the usual bustle of the city centre. She'd called and texted Simon, but he wasn't answering. She'd have to follow him.

Come on, Jill.

Florence expected her assistant to appear in something small and cute. A pink Mini or a small green Fiat.

That wasn't the case.

A monstrous pickup truck, midnight black, came to a stop at the side of the road. Florence didn't pay any attention to it at first. It was impossible to imagine tiny Jill at the wheel of such a vehicle. Then the pickup's horn startled her.

"Over here, Florence."

"Jill?" Florence scrambled to her feet and hurried over. The vehicle was enormous, with two rows of seats and a huge flatbed at the back. She got in the front passenger seat.

"This is your ride?"

Jill grinned. "I grew up on a farm, so I got used to driving a pickup."

It was clean inside, and looked to be a pretty new vehicle. Jill turned down the rock music playing on the radio.

"Were you able to sneak out of the office?" Florence said.

Jill nodded. "I had to leave my coat behind. Your father kept asking me where you were, and if I had heard from you."

"I hope you told him nothing."

"Nothing. Just like you said." Jill frowned. "But I felt bad about lying."

Florence waved her hand impatiently. "Never mind that. I need you for something important."

"What's the big secret?"

"We have to take a field trip."

"Great!"

"We're going to Claremorris."

"In Mayo? That's the other side of the country."

Florence was relieved Jill knew that much. "This is very important."

"Oh, that's where your friend's birthday party is."

"I told you about that?"

Jill blushed a little. "Um, no, but I saw it on your Instagram feed. You posted a photo of the invitation."

Florence stared at her assistant evenly. "You follow me on the Gram?"

"Under a different name." Jill blushed even deeper, then forced a laugh. "I spend too much time online."

What a nerd, Florence thought. She said, "Let's get going. It's urgent."

The journey would take about two and a half hours and Simon had a head start. Florence figured he'd be safe while he was on the road. The hotel would probably be the real danger zone. Anonymous. Full of strangers. Hopefully the hitman wouldn't realise Simon had left Dublin.

Jill pulled out into traffic.

She headed towards the River Liffey, across the bridge to the south quays, then drove along the quays heading west.

The historic Four Courts building reared up on the other side of the river. Florence stared at it, taking in the sight of the neoclassical structure, with its copper dome.

"Why is it called The Four Courts anyway?" Florence said with a scowl. "I mean, surely there are more than four courtrooms."

She wasn't expecting an answer, but Jill began to speak enthusiastically.

"It comes from the old British system. There were the four courts of Chancery, King's Bench, Exchequer and Common Pleas. Now we have the High Court, the Court of Appeal, Dublin Circuit Court and the Supreme—"

"Okay, okay. I don't actually care."

Florence felt sick thinking of all the laws she must be breaking.

"Why do you know so much about the courts?"

"They say you should know your enemy." Jill gave a nervous laugh.

"Your enemy?"

"The state. The authorities. I guess I'd call myself a libertarian. I used to be an anarchist, but I'm a bit more moderate now."

"Okay," Florence said with just enough scorn to make sure Jill would stop talking politics.

"This is going to be fun," Jill said after a moment.

"Do you know the way?"

"Pretty much. That farm where I grew up? It was in Galway."

Not far from Claremorris.

"Good," Florence said.

Traffic forced them to slow as they approached Euston Station, one of the city's main train stations.

"How do you like farms?" Florence asked.

"Not much. I have pretty bad hay fever? I stayed indoors whenever I could and played computer games. Drove my grandparents crazy."

"What about your parents?"

Jill looked at Florence. "Oh, they, uh, they weren't really—"

Just then an old lady stepped off the footpath and out onto the road in front of them.

Florence shouted, "Watch out!"

Jill saw the woman and wrenched the wheel to the side. They veered out into the other lane. Luckily, there were no cars coming at them. Jill brought the truck to a stop.

"Wow," Jill gasped. "That was a close one. Are you okay?"

Florence didn't reply. Instead, she jumped out of the truck, intending to give the pedestrian a piece of her mind. She noticed that a crowd on the footpath had stopped to stare.

Jill eased the pickup truck back into the correct lane and pulled in at the kerb. Amazingly, the pedestrian who had nearly got herself killed walked right past Florence, heading towards the truck. Florence trotted after her.

"Hello," she called. "Excuse me?"

The woman ignored Florence, and rapped her knuckles on the truck's passenger window. Florence could see people on the footpath looking at her.

Mocking her.

Enough, Florence told herself.

The passenger window powered down and the woman leaned in. Florence came up behind her, irritated to see that Jill was already engrossed in conversation.

Good god. Was Jill actually laughing?

"Excuse me. What do you think you're doing?" Florence said as loud as she could.

The woman turned around. A large lady, grey curly hair. Not as old as Florence had thought first. In her fifties or sixties. It was hard to tell. She had a fleshy pink face and a heaving bosom that pulled Florence's eyes to it involuntarily. She was short and stout, built like a Doberman. She wore light cotton pants, a pink blouse and sensible shoes.

The woman smiled.

"Oh, hello. I'm Kim."

"I don't care what your name is, you dummy."

Kim turned back to Jill, giving no sign that she'd heard Florence.

Jill said, "This lady just missed her train, but she's headed our way. I told her we can give her a lift."

"No," Florence said. "I don't think so."

Again the woman gave no sign of hearing. She opened the front passenger door and settled herself in Florence's seat.

Jill shot her an apologetic look. "Um, there's plenty of legroom in the back, Florence?"

Florence would have argued but the clock was ticking. After a moment's hesitation, she got in the back seat.

"Fine. Let's go."

"Yes, let's go," Kim said. "Buckle up, girls."

CHAPTER FORTY

Kinnegad, Friday, 3:30 pm.
Simon and Hazel were seated across from each other at a picnic bench. They were outside a pub in the small town of Kinnegad in Westmeath. From where they sat, they could look up at the side of the local church.

They hadn't been on the road long, but Simon was hungry, having missed lunch because of his trip to the jewellery shop. Now he was eating a toasted cheese and ham sandwich. A few locals had gathered at nearby benches, sinking beers in the afternoon sun. Simon slathered hot English mustard onto his sandwich and bit into it.

"I wonder if Ronan still collects beer mats," Hazel said.

She stirred sugar into her skinny cappuccino and slipped on a pair of huge movie star shades.

"I forgot about that," Simon said. "He must have a million by now."

"He'd need a room to store them all in."

"Well, him and Deb don't have any children, so maybe he has enough space for his collection."

Hazel downed half her coffee in one go. "Deb never gave me maternal vibes."

Simon had to agree. He'd never really warmed to Ronan's wife, and he wasn't sure why. Maybe it was just her quiet intensity behind them. Deb was a detective in the Gardaí. It was her transfer to Claremorris that forced Ronan to leave Dublin.

Simon finished the sandwich. He felt exhausted rather than satisfied. Maybe his taste buds were to blame, but he felt he might as well have put mustard on a beer mat.

Hazel downed the last of her coffee.

"Ready to go?" Simon asked.

Hazel nodded. "I just want to use the toilet first."

"I'll wait by the car."

Simon watched her go, then wiped his hands on a napkin and got to his feet. The beer garden spilled out onto the pub's car park. He walked towards Hazel's car and stood leaning against it.

The sun beat down mercilessly. Simon could feel the perspiration under his arms. He closed his eyes for a moment. Kept them shut until he heard footsteps approaching.

He opened them to see Hazel. She looked fabulous in the bright light. There was a vibrancy about her. Something energetic about her tanned skin. Her full lips. Had she put on some lipstick? She'd certainly put her hair in a high ponytail.

Hazel walked up to Simon. She pressed one hand against his chest, and put her lips close to his ear. He froze in surprise, the car's body hot against his back, her hand hot against his heart.

Hazel whispered, "I'm glad you dumped her."

Simon was too surprised to say anything, even when her hand slid down his belly and stopped at his belt.

She leaned in slowly, and said, "Very glad."

CHAPTER FORTY-ONE

Dublin, Friday, 3:31 pm.
Fuming in the backseat of the pickup truck, Florence felt like a child being driven to the dentist's surgery. Kim smelled of cat and Florence could see hairs all over the shoulders of her blouse.

"What were you doing back there?" Florence said. "Trying to get yourself killed?"

The lady laughed. She laughed at everything.

"I got into such a state when I missed my train," Kim said. "I didn't know what I was doing. The next one wasn't for two hours, and I knew that would be too late. So I wandered out of the station, wondering what I should do. I was thinking about how much a taxi would cost."

"To Claremorris? A taxi would cost an absolute fortune," Jill said with a smile.

"I think you're right." Kim chuckled.

Florence rolled her eyes, though she knew neither of the two women in the front would see it.

"And then you stepped out onto the road like a lemming?" Florence prompted.

Kim turned her head a little and glanced back. "I feel awfully stupid. I suppose my mind was wandering."

"What exactly are you doing in Claremorris?"

Jill flinched at the harshness of Florence's tone, but she kept her eye on the road and said nothing. Ever since the near miss, she'd been doing a better job of paying attention to her driving.

Kim said, "I'm going to a party."

"So are we!" Jill said. "I mean Florence is. I'm just driving her."

Kim cocked an eyebrow. "At Fitzgerald's Hotel?"

Jill shrugged. "I don't know, actually. Florence?"

"Yes. You know Ronan?"

The woman chuckled. "Indeed. I'm his aunt. And he's a popular lad too. I'm sure there are many Dubs heading west for the night."

Florence nodded slowly. It was true that Ronan was popular. He probably would have dozens of people heading from Dublin to Claremorris to usher in his fiftieth. Simon had said that a number of former colleagues were travelling down for the night.

Kim said, "I don't remember him mentioning any Florence to me."

The audacity of this woman. Kim now sounded suspicious of Florence, as if Florence was telling fibs.

"The invitation would have been under my boyfriend's name. Simon Hill."

"Oh, Simon. I thought he was going alone."

Kim smiled and looked out the window.

Though she was angry, Florence decided she wasn't going to say another word to this woman for the rest of the journey.

She took out her phone and rang Fitzgerald's. She supposed she'd better book a room.

CHAPTER FORTY-TWO

Dublin, Friday, 3:32 pm.

Monotony set in as Thomas Ogden left the city centre behind and headed out of Dublin. He found that there was little to see from the motorway. Just green hills. Roundabouts. Farms and fields.

But Thomas didn't feel bored. The kill lay ahead of him and the desire to get it done lit a fire inside him. If he liked, he could do the job now. On the road. He could make it look like a traffic accident. It was pleasant to visualise the possibilities.

But he thought he'd wait until the hotel.

When he arrived in Dublin, he hadn't been sure the birthday party was still on the agenda. His target might have remained in Dublin. But no. It was still on.

As he drove, he phoned Wendy.

"Bad news, honey. I think it's going to be tomorrow before I get home."

"Oh, Thomas."

"I know, I know. I'll make it up to you. Don't forget about our holiday. Have you decided where you want to go?"

"I'm thinking of Kenya," Wendy said.

So she had started researching the trip. There was excitement in her voice.

"Really?"

"Don't you think it would be interesting?"

Thomas frowned. "Interesting? Sure. Just a little dangerous, don't you think?"

"You're obsessed with safety. You know that? You always think something awful is going to happen."

"Because awful things happen every day. We have a child."

"Wherever we go, we'll be careful. That's all you can do. After that, you just have to trust god."

"Uh huh."

"Thomas?"

"Yes?"

"I love you."

He smiled. "I love you too, Wendy."

"I'm trusting you. You... you'd never betray that trust, would you? You'd never lie to me?"

"Of course not. What do you mean?"

"All these business trips. I know it's crazy, but sometimes I'm afraid there's another woman."

Thomas laughed. "God, no. Why would you think that? Just because I go away once in a while?"

"And you seem so distracted. Always on your computer and checking your phone."

He'd have to do something about that. Reign his activities in a little. Before they took over his whole life. He used to be an ordinary guy, who dabbled in crime. But maybe he was becoming a killer who dabbled in being ordinary.

"You have nothing to worry about. Everything will be okay, Wendy. You'll see."

"I miss you, Thomas."

"I'll get home as soon as I can."

He ended the call. An exit ramp appeared ahead. Thomas saw a sign for a shop, one of those huge home and garden stores, just a mile off the motorway. They ought to have a good selection of tools. He took the turn, deciding that he could afford a quick detour.

CHAPTER FORTY-THREE

Claremorris, Friday, 5:45 pm.
Claremorris is a small town with a population of three or four thousand people. Simon had been there before once. He mostly remembered the farmland and the narrow country roads. Fitzgerald's Hotel lay off the motorway, about a mile from the train station. Hazel pulled into the sprawling car park and found a space.

Simon's chest had been hammering the whole way here, ever since Hazel's flirtation in the pub car park. During the rest of the journey, she acted as if nothing had happened, but the tension between them crackled in the air until it was unbearable.

Simon got out of the car. The hotel was big in the way a lot of rural hotels are big. Land was cheap, so they'd built plenty of rooms and a nice big parking area.

Simon grabbed his overnight bag from the backseat and Hazel's too. He followed Hazel as she started towards the entrance.

Simon watched her hips. He'd always thought there was something sensual about the way Hazel walked. A rhythm that spoke to him. As if sensing his thoughts, she ran a hand through her hair. Simon watched it tumble down her back.

The hotel's automatic doors swung open. They stepped into the lobby. It was all bright lights, wooden fixtures and ferny plants. Very nice. A 4-star hotel, Ronan had said.

And there he was.

Ronan and his wife stood in the middle of the lobby greeting another couple. Ronan was a big man with a barrel chest and a full, a chestnut-coloured beard that joined seamlessly with the hair on his head.

His wife looked rake-thin compared to Ronan, though Deb's build was actually average. She liked to jog when she wasn't on duty.

Ronan caught sight of Simon and Hazel and excused himself from the couple he was speaking to. He started towards them, with Deb following right behind.

"This warms my heart," Ronan said, glancing at them and then at Deb. "The old crew is back together. This is perfect."

"Hello, Ronan," Hazel said.

"Hazel, how are you? Where's the golfer? Barry, isn't it?"

"Gary," Hazel said. "He didn't make the cut. I dropped him on the fifth hole."

Ronan winced. "Ouch. It's a rare man who can keep up with you."

He and Simon shook hands. Ronan pulled him into a bear hug, while Deb hugged Hazel.

"Where's her ladyship?" Ronan said, in a discreet voice. "Is she waiting to be announced by her maids?"

Simon forced a smile. "Florence and I split up."

"I'm sorry," Deb said.

But Simon caught the look that passed between Deb and Ronan. "What?"

Ronan shrugged. "Nothing. It's just that… you know, Florence is a little…"

"What?"

"You know, high maintenance."

Simon felt heat come into his face. Had everyone been waiting for his relationship to fall apart?

"I better check in," Simon said. "I need a shower."

Ronan nodded. "You got it, pal. Come back down when you're ready. We have the function room from seven o'clock. There'll be food, there'll be nibbles. It's perfect."

"Sure," Simon said.

He and Hazel checked in, then walked across the lobby to the elevator together.

CHAPTER FORTY-FOUR

London, Friday, 6:01 pm.
In the bedroom, Archie Browne was dressing. He struggled, but finally got the bow tie done. At least, he thought he did. But when Lucinda came into the room, she pulled it off him and tied it properly.

"After all these years," she said, with a shake of her head.

Archie grinned.

"I love being married," he said.

Lucinda helped him get his jacket on, then turned her back so he could close the clasp on her necklace. Archie's arthritis made it tricky, but he got it in the end.

"You grow more beautiful every day," Archie said.

"Liar."

He shook his head. "No lie."

Lucinda's looks had changed during their decades together. She'd started to appear more distinguished, wiser. Foxier, he'd told her one night. She'd laughed it off, but he meant it. She was sixty, a little younger than him, and a hell of a lot smarter. Without her in his life, he probably would have done something stupid by now.

He stole a glance at his iPhone while Lucinda fussed with her hair. It was the latest model, and he loved it. In fact, he loved pretty much any gadget. If only his ancestors in the West Indies and rural Ireland could have imagined the technological marvels of today. They would have thought it was magic.

"I hope you're not going to play with that thing all night," Lucinda said.

"Absolutely not," Archie said and set it down on the dresser. He wouldn't play with it, but he'd have to check in on what was happening in Ireland.

He followed Lucinda to the dining room, made his way over to the drinks cabinet.

"A little brandy, Lucinda?"

She cocked an eyebrow, but didn't say no. Archie poured two glasses. Evening sun streamed in the window. If only he could stay in this moment forever. But bad things happened in the world. He knew that better than anyone.

His phone buzzed, just as he and Lucinda were clinking their glasses together.

"It can wait," she told him.

There was that wisdom again.

"I bet you're right," Archie said. He wished he could check it all the same. It was hard to relax, to take his mind off the injustices he saw every day, all over the world. Sometimes he didn't know what to work on first. He'd always wanted to go to Barbados, to see the land of his ancestors and help their descendants, a few hundred Red Legs who still lived in poverty.

But there were so many other struggles.

So many other people who needed help.

He thought back to his days presiding over the magistrate's court. On the rare occasion a black barrister appeared in the courtroom, the court staff generally mistook them for a defendant. Archie envied all those old, white, upper-class men. They were who they were. Nice and simple. But his identity had been formed by the spaces between categories. Sometimes he wasn't sure where he belonged.

Thank God for Lucinda. When he felt down, she was the only thing that could help. Did more for his mood than lithium ever had.

"What are you thinking about, Archie?"

"Just reflecting on how much I love you," he said.

His wife smiled. "That's alright then," she said.

CHAPTER FORTY-FIVE

Claremorris. Friday, 6:10 pm.

Simon walked past room 309 and followed Hazel to the door of 308. He waited as she unlocked it, stepped inside and slid her card into the slot on the wall. The lights came on. It was a spacious room, with a king-size bed, big TV, and a door to the adjoining room. Simon set Hazel's bag down at the foot of her bed.

"I better go get cleaned up," Simon said.

"Okay." Hazel pushed open the bathroom door and looked inside. "See you later."

Simon backed out of the room. Disappointment bubbled up inside. Hadn't she wanted him to stay? All that tension between them during the journey. He was sure he hadn't imagined it, sparking between them. To just say goodbye seemed an anti-climax.

He unlocked the door to his own room and stepped inside. It was a mirror-image of Hazel's. The same bed. The same bathroom.

And a door to the adjoining room. Hazel's room.

Simon unlocked the door on his side. After a small gap, there was another door. He knocked his knuckles on the wood.

The door opened and Hazel was framed in the doorway. She'd let her hair down. Simon thought she'd never looked so good.

"I love adjoining hotel rooms," Hazel said.

She was in Simon's arms before he could reply. Her body pressed against his, her tongue hot as it darted into his mouth.

She jumped up and he caught her. Her legs cinched around his waist. He staggered forward and they fell on the bed. Their teeth smashed together, but neither of them paused.

"You're sure?" Hazel said between hungry kisses.

He didn't need to think. Florence was history.

"I'm sure," he gasped.

Hazel unfastened his belt and pulled down his trousers. Then she was slipping out of her clothes too and Simon stopped thinking about Florence.

CHAPTER FORTY-SIX

Claremorris. Friday, 6:35 pm.
Jill brought the pickup truck to a halt in front of Fitzgerald's Hotel. Florence felt like the journey had taken years, rather than a few hours. If Jill's overcautious driving hadn't been enough, Kim's presence had made the journey seem even longer.

She'd talked endlessly about her early retirement and her love of car engines and her cat, Bony, for at least a hundred kilometres. It was like she hadn't talked to anyone for a year. If Kim loved cars so much, Florence wondered why she didn't have her own. Why did she need to take the train?

During the last hour of the journey, Kim had reclined her seat and fallen asleep. She snored even louder than Simon. At a sharp bend in the road, her handbag had tipped over out of her lap. Jill caught it with one hand, but nearly crashed the pickup while she was at it. She fumbled with the bag, then passed it back to Kim.

Now that they had arrived, Kim stretched and yawned.

Florence opened the door and got out. She could smell cut grass on the air. Hay too. And animals not far away. This place really was in the sticks.

Kim stepped out of the truck.

"Do you want to split the cost of a room?" she said. "They often have rooms with two or three beds. We could save money by sharing."

"I don't think so," Florence said.

The only reason she'd booked a room was to placate Jill. She wasn't going to have Kim tagging along with her for the whole trip, even if she was Ronan's aunt. Soon she'd be angling for free drinks and asking for a lift back to Dublin the next day.

No thanks.

Kim didn't seem to notice Florence's answer.

"Shall we go in?" she said.

Jill got out from behind the driver's seat. "You go ahead," she said. "We'll be there soon."

Kim hesitated.

"Go on," Florence snapped.

"Okay, see you inside."

Kim ambled towards the hotel entrance.

Florence shook her head. She said, "I was afraid you'd let her tag along. I thought you liked her. You two were chatting for a long time."

Jill came and stood close to Florence. She whispered, "To be honest, I feel like there's something off about Kim."

"You mean the way she stepped out on the road? And just happened to be coming here?"

Jill said, "By itself, I wouldn't mind that. I mean, we *were* passing the train station. She really could have missed her train."

Florence nodded impatiently. She was tired after the drive, but eager to find Simon. There were only four hours left. She retrieved her laptop bag from the backseat.

"Okay. It's possible."

"Yeah," Jill said. "But then when her bag tipped over, I saw inside it. I saw her phone."

"So what?"

"So this nice old lady has a KryptX."

Florence sighed. "What the hell is that?"

"It's an encrypted phone made in Austria. It's billed as the ultimate encrypted untraceable phone. Very secure. Very high-tech. And extremely expensive."

Florence hesitated. "Why would Ronan's batty aunt have one of those things?"

"That's what I asked myself. She must have some pretty important traffic passing through that phone. Stuff she wants no one else to see. And I don't think it's her bingo scores."

"I wonder what she's up to," Florence said.

Jill reached into her pocket and pulled out a bricklike phone in a rubber case.

"Me too. That's why I took her phone."

CHAPTER FORTY-SEVEN

Claremorris, Friday, 6:39 pm.
Thomas swung the rental car into the hotel car park. He spotted Florence Lynch right away. She stood next to a pickup truck, an expression on her face like she'd just been slapped with a bag of lemons. A young woman with black hair came around the back of the truck. This must be her personal assistant, Thomas figured. Jill Fitzgibbon.

He pulled into a parking space on the far side of the lot. In the mirror, he checked himself. Everything still looked good. The baseball cap. The black T-shirt. The shades. He ran his hands over the claw hammer he'd bought at the hardware shop. He couldn't wait to use it.

The two women went inside the hotel. Florence Lynch must want to make a last-ditch effort to save her relationship. Thomas could have told her it was too late for that. Ever since she'd hired him, it was too late.

He was preparing himself to go in when his phone rang. It was Wendy.

"Hello darling. I can't really talk right now."

There was a pause. He could hear Wendy breathing. Then she said, in a very deliberate voice, like she was reading from a script, "The police are here, Thomas. They want to speak to you."

CHAPTER FORTY-EIGHT

Claremorris. Friday, 6:43 pm.
Florence hurried Jill into the hotel lobby, dragging her by the elbow. At a glance, she took in the fake plants, cheap Ikea furnishings, and tasteless ceiling lights. Florence shook her head, distractedly.

It was just like Simon's friend to choose somewhere tacky and bland. Florence hated hotels that were anything less than five stars. She still remembered Simon being surprised when she mentioned a six-star luxury hotel she had stayed in once.

"I thought five was the maximum?" he'd said with a confused expression.

"Can you slow down?" Jill hissed, as she scrambled to keep up.

But Florence couldn't. She caught sight of Kim at the reception desk. The older woman was accepting a key card.

"Kim?" Florence called.

"Hello girls."

"What room are you in? We can catch up later, before the party."

"Great idea. I'm in 325."

"Perfect," Florence said.

"And you?"

"I don't know. We'll call to your room once we've all had a chance to get refreshed."

Kim nodded. Florence could see the disappointment on her face. She wanted to know where Florence was staying. Maybe Jill was right to be suspicious of her.

Florence turned her attention to the lady behind the check-in desk. While the booking was processed, Florence watched Kim walk down the corridor, her handbag slung over her shoulder.

Moving very slowly. Lingering.

"Florence?"

She spun around to see a big bear of a man in a close-fitting three-piece suit. Ronan had grown larger since he left Dublin. The formal clothes made him look like he was getting married rather than simply celebrating his birthday.

"Hello, Ronan." She turned her smile on at full blast. "Good to see you. Happy birthday."

They hugged briefly, each of them standing well back. Florence air-kissed each cheek. She had no intention of letting Ronan's beard scratch her face. It was liable to set off her eczema and that would take weeks to calm down.

"I wasn't expecting you," Ronan said hesitantly. He gave Jill a curious smile. "Hello."

They shook hands.

"Jill is my PA," Florence explained.

The crinkle in Ronan's brow only deepened.

Florence accepted her key card from the receptionist and turned to Ronan.

"Have you seen Simon?" she said.

Ronan nodded slowly.

"Sure," he said.

"What room is he in?"

"I don't know." He lowered his voice. "He said you... I thought you might not be coming."

"It's just a misunderstanding."

"Oh. Perfect."

"Simon and I are solid."

"Perfect," Ronan said. "My mistake."

Florence caught sight of a wiry woman talking to other arrivals on the far side of the lobby. Deb, Ronan's wife.

The detective.

Florence had completely forgotten that there was a law enforcement presence.

She wanted to ask the receptionist what room Simon was in, but even more than that she wanted to get away from Deb. She was sure guilt was written all over her face and Deb would read it at a glance.

"See you later," Florence said.

Ronan nodded.

Jill said, "By the way, we gave your aunt a lift."

"My aunt?" Ronan chuckled. "I think you're mistaken. Sadly, I don't have any aunt."

CHAPTER FORTY-NINE

Claremorris, Friday, 6:45 pm.
Thomas Ogden had always known this moment may come. He leaned back in the driver's seat of the rental car. With the phone pressed to his ear, he stared at the hotel. The evening sun reflected off its windows, making it look like the building was in flames.

"Are you still there?" Wendy asked.

"Yes."

He heard her take in a sharp breath. "A second constable has just arrived. They want to speak to you."

"What's this about? I'm really quite busy. Surely it's some mistake?"

"Thomas." Her voice broke. "Do you know anything about a man being killed last night? Were you involved in it in any way?"

He forced a laugh.

"What are you talking about? We watched that silly movie last night."

"Earlier. They found your wallet near a man's body. His name is – was – Brook Reynolds."

So that was where his wallet had gone. He'd taken so many elaborate precautions, used so many sophisticated security features to hide his digital footprint. Then a misplaced wallet tied a noose around his neck.

"Don't be silly," Thomas said. "My wallet is missing. I discovered that this morning. A pickpocket must have taken it. What have they told you?"

"They talked to your boss. She says you're not on a business trip. She thought you were at home in bed sick."

"Yeah, but that's… I can explain. Just—"

"Oh, Thomas."

The police were probably running a trace. How long would it take to find his location? To co-ordinate with their Irish counterparts and get officers on the scene?

"I'm sorry, Wendy," he said. "I'm going into a meeting. Let's talk about this later."

He ended the call, realising he was drenched in sweat. He shifted uncomfortably, panic creeping up his throat. He took a breath, trying to steady his racing pulse.

This is it, he thought. *The end.*

On the upside, it was also a new beginning. Thomas had a fake ID and a nice nest egg in bitcoin, which could be accessed from anywhere in the world. He needed to get out of the country as soon as possible. And he couldn't go back to the UK.

Thomas thought of that quote from Samuel Johnson.

Sir, when a man is tired of London, he is tired of life; for there is in London all that life can afford.

Thomas wasn't tired of it. He would have liked to stay, but sometimes fate forces your hand.

A few seconds searching Google established that an airport called Ireland West Airport Knock was only 26 kilometres away. He could ditch the rental car there and fly to Cologne. From Germany, he'd have easy access to the rest of the European mainland.

It would be hard to live without his family. He was a survivor, though. In time, Thomas knew he'd adapt. Maybe he could persuade Wendy to follow him. He could make her understand. And as a Christian, she was basically duty-bound to forgive him.

He'd head to the airport as soon as he completed the current job.

10:44 pm had been his deadline, but that was far too late now.

He needed to kill the target immediately.

CHAPTER FIFTY

Claremorris. Friday, 7:00 pm.

Florence dragged Jill towards the stairs.

"What are you doing?" Jill hissed. "You should tell your friend someone is pretending to be his aunt."

"Later," Florence said. As she led the way up the staircase, she glanced at her key card. It was for room 326. She realised they were in the room next to Kim. She wondered if the hotel booked guests into rooms next to each other to make it easier for housekeeping. It would be just like a cheap place like this to be so mercenary.

On the third floor, they entered their room and closed the door. There were two double beds, a desk, a TV and a couple of chairs. The window looked out onto the car park. Jill set her bag down on the desk.

"May I?" she asked, opening the minibar.

Florence nodded.

Jill grabbed a Pepsi, took a long drink of it, then perched on the nearest bed. Florence realised she was thirsty too, and she was finally starting to feel hungry. She grabbed a bottle of water from the fridge.

"What's going on here?" Jill said. "Encrypted phones, false identities. Did I just step into an Ian Fleming story?"

She looked rather pleased.

"Keep your voice down," Florence hissed. It was one of those hotels with interconnecting rooms. There was a door which led to the next room. Florence hated hotels with this feature. Handy for a family or a group of friends. But right now, Florence was worried about the sound of their voices carrying into Kim's room.

She thought for a moment. She had to tell Jill something.

"This is going to sound crazy."

"I'm listening," Jill said.

"Simon's life is in danger."

"What?"

Florence nodded. "Someone wants to kill him."

"What makes you think that?"

Florence said, "I got an anonymous tip."

"That's bizarre. And you think it's for real?"

"I think so."

"Did you report it yet? We better call someone." Jill's eyes lit up. "I know, we can tell Deb. You said she's a detective, right?"

"We are not telling Deb or anyone else anything. Do you understand me?"

"What? Why?"

"The tip warned me to trust no one." Florence could see Jill was about to argue with her. Quickly she said, "We need to fix this. You and me."

"How?"

"I wish that stupid client was here. The tech guy. Jon Glynn. Maybe he could get Kim's phone unlocked."

But I was a jerk to him, so I lost the work. Nice going, Florence.

Jill smiled. "I'm a much better hacker than Jon Glynn."

Florence stared at her PA as if seeing her for the first time. She looked about ten years old. But determination shone in her eyes.

"What makes you think that?"

Jill said, "Well, I was able to get into his system."

"Jon Glynn's? How?"

"It would take a long time to explain, but—"

"Never mind how. I meant *why*?"

Jill shrugged. "For the challenge." She paused. "I hack into every client's system. It's nothing malicious. It's just satisfying."

Florence was amazed.

"Why are you a PA if you're such a great hacker?"

"Well, no one's meant to know what a great hacker I am. I don't advertise it. And secondly, part of the reason your dad hired me was to keep an eye on you."

"What?"

"When he was interviewing me, I mentioned that I like technology. He said you were terrible at computers and he didn't want you messing things up."

I messed things up alright.

"How quickly can you get into that phone?"

"A thousand years?" Jill said. "That's what the manufacturer claims."

"Oh god."

Jill smiled. "But these things are never as tight as they say. I've heard a rumour that a vulnerability has been found already."

"Can you check it out?"

"Sure."

Florence slipped her laptop out of its case, together with its power cable. She set it down on the table and plugged it in.

Jill looked around in her own handbag and pulled out her phone's charger cable. She plugged one end into Kim's encrypted phone and the other end into Florence's laptop. She sat down in front of the laptop as it booted up.

Jill said, "Wait, so you think *Kim* is going to kill Simon? But she's, like, a grandmother. It can't be her. Why would she do that?"

Florence shook her head.

"Being older doesn't mean you're good," she said. "You know, you hear of those doctors and nurses who murder patients for decades and no one notices?"

"Um. I guess."

"Well, there you go."

The laptop finished booting. Florence stared at her wallpaper – a photo of her and Simon.

"And here we go," Jill said, as she began tapping on keys.

CHAPTER FIFTY-ONE

Claremorris. Friday, 7:05 pm.
Hazel snuggled into the crook of Simon's arm. For a moment she kept her eyes closed, just wanting to enjoy the feeling. The duvet lay on the floor next to the bed. The room was so warm, it wasn't needed. They were both naked.

"You know what I'd love now?" Simon said.

"A cigarette?"

"God, no. I have no idea why anyone would want a cigarette after sex. I want a milkshake. Mint flavour."

Hazel laughed and ran her hand over the dark curls on Simon's chest. His body was lean, but skinnier than she had thought. No muscle. No six-pack. More like a zero-pack.

The excitement had worn off. Hazel was underwhelmed.

At first, she had enjoyed having Simon. The pleasure was nothing to do with Simon himself, who seemed entirely clueless about female anatomy. All the pleasure came from taking what was Florence's. *That* was fun.

"Mint?" Hazel said. "I hate mint ice cream."

Simon disentangled himself from her and sat up in the bed. A used condom lay on the sheet beside him. Picking it up between his thumb and forefinger, he lobbed it across the room towards the bin, but it fell short, splattering on the floor next to the basket. He picked up the phone next to the bed. Hazel listened while he ordered from room service.

"Want anything?" Simon said.

"No. I'll have a drink when we go downstairs."

"That's all," Simon said into the receiver. He put the phone down and hugged Hazel again. "I'd forgotten about the party. We don't have to go down, you know. I don't mind. I just want to be with you."

Hazel smiled.

"I'd like to go down," she said. "We've come all this way."

"I don't know if I can keep my hands off you."

"Who said you should?"

Hazel wanted everyone to see her and Simon together. Word might get back to Florence.

CHAPTER FIFTY-TWO

Claremorris. Friday, 7:10 pm.

Thomas entered the hotel. He had his bag slung over his shoulder. The new hammer was inside it. His phone was in his hand, the GPS tracker on the screen. Sending him towards the target. He made his way quickly across the floor to the reception desk. The young woman behind the desk looked up.

"Good evening, sir."

Thomas did his best to look alarmed. "There's a fire in the bin outside. Do you have an extinguisher?"

"A fire? Are you sure?"

He was sure. He'd started it himself.

While she hurried outside to check, Thomas leapt over the counter.

The tracker on his phone gave him a pretty good idea where the target was. But time was of the essence, so he wanted to check the room number. It only took a few seconds to find it on the computer.

Then he was on his way upstairs.

CHAPTER FIFTY-THREE

Claremorris. Friday, 7:11 pm.

Kim emptied everything out onto the bed. Her make-up, umbrella, tissues, paracetamol. The gun. The grenade. But no phone. It definitely wasn't there. She looked at all her bits and bobs laid out on the clean white duvet. She couldn't understand it.

Had the phone fallen out of her bag? Maybe it was on the floor of the pickup truck. Falling asleep had been a bad idea. But it wasn't like she planned that. It had just happened.

"Fuck," she shouted.

Imperator wasn't going to be happy. Not that he could do much to her. Not with a death sentence already hanging over her head. But failure wasn't the note she wanted to go out on.

Where the hell was the phone?

CHAPTER FIFTY-FOUR

Claremorris. Friday, 7:12 pm.

Sitting at the writing table next to the TV, Jill stopped tapping at the keyboard.

"Got it," she said. "I'm in."

Florence pulled herself away from the window. She had been staring out at the surrounding fields, reflecting on how badly everything had gone. Now she hurried to Jill's side.

Jill said, "I had to buy some code, just to hurry things along. I assume you're good for it? Seven hundred euro?"

"Buy some code?" *How do you buy code?* Florence shook her head. "Yeah, fine. Whatever. You're in. That's all I care about. So what have we got?"

Jill unplugged the phone from the computer.

"Let's check it out."

She began scrolling through it. Florence watched impatiently. She was tempted to snatch the device out of Jill's hands.

"Interesting," Jill said. "There's some kind of tracker app. I wonder what it's tracking. There are three dots on the map. Let me zoom in. They're all really close."

"One of them must be Simon," Florence said.

"One is down the hall, and around the corner." Jill pinched the map between her fingers, zooming in. She smiled. "This is a really good tracker."

"You can fangirl over it later," Florence snapped.

She walked over to the window. She felt almost numb with terror. It was impossible for her to remain still. She looked out at the fields stretching into the distance. It looked so peaceful.

"Um, Florence."

"Yes?"

"Do you have your phone on you?"

Florence was holding it in her hand. "Yeah. Why?"

"Because one of the dots on this screen just moved."

"What?"

"It moved when you walked across the room."

"You mean Kim was tracking *me*? Tracking my phone?"

Jill nodded. "Looks like it."

"I don't understand why she'd do that. And who's the third dot?"

"No idea," Jill said.

Florence walked back to Jill's side. "Anyway, we now know that Kim did find us deliberately in

Dublin. She must have been waiting for us by the station. A missed train was probably the best excuse she could come up with."

"She must have been watching like a hawk. Checking the tracker and watching each car approaching."

Florence said, "I need to talk to her."

Suddenly Kim's voice came from the next room. "Fuck."

Jill gave a lopsided smile. "I guess she found out she's lost her phone."

Florence looked at her PA. In that moment, with her big grin, she looked even younger than her twenty-one years. She looked like a kid. Florence said, "I'm sorry for getting you mixed up in this."

"Are you kidding?" Jill said. "This is exciting. But I wish you'd tell me what's really going on."

Florence sighed.

"Someone hired a hitman to kill Simon. That's all I know."

Jill stared at her. "That's pretty wild."

"Yes, it is. And time is running out." Florence took a breath and thought. She said, "Okay. Here's what we're going to do."

Florence set out the plan. Jill wasn't enthusiastic about it, but Florence really didn't care.

She threw her phone down on the bed and got her bottle of Chanel from her handbag. She left Jill where she was, and stepped out into the hallway, closing the door behind her. A couple of steps brought her to the door of the next room.

Florence knocked on Kim's door.

Her pulse throbbed in her ears as she waited.

The sound of footsteps came from the other side of the door. Kim opened up with a sour expression on her face. Sourness turned to confusion when she saw Florence.

"What are you—"

Florence sprayed perfume into the older woman's eyes. Kim shrieked and stumbled backwards, trying to get away. Florence stepped into the room after her. She closed the door and sprayed more Chanel in Kim's face. Kim shouted even louder, rubbing wildly at her eyes.

Florence went over to the interconnecting door, leading to her own room. She opened it up. Jill stood on the other side with a length of electrical cable in her hands. Florence could see one of the bedside lamps lying on the floor, with the mutilated wire cut off.

Kim staggered blindly across the room, trying to get to the bathroom. Florence got in her way, pushed her down onto the bed.

"What are you doing? This is *assault*."

With some effort, Florence turned Kim over on her belly and pulled her hands behind her back. Jill tied her wrists together with the cable. They ignored Kim's howls of pain.

"If you don't shut up, I'm going to gag you," Florence said.

"This is crazy."

"Shut up. Just cooperate and we won't hurt you."

Florence caught Jill's startled expression. Florence hadn't said anything about hurting anyone. But she'd do whatever she had to.

The faint ping of the elevator came from down the corridor.

Florence and Jill both looked at each other. Things had gone so crazy so quickly that everything sounded suspicious, even a lift.

Footsteps approached.

Was it Simon coming? No. The steps were heavy, deliberate. It didn't sound like a maid either. Ronan?

"Let me up, let me go," Kim gasped.

Florence grabbed a pillow and slipped it out of the case.

"Open her mouth."

Jill forced Kim's mouth open, and Florence stuffed the pillowcase inside.

The footsteps on the corridor were getting closer. Suddenly they stopped. Very close by. Not outside this room, but outside the other one.

Florence ran to the interconnecting door and closed it quietly. It clicked shut a moment before the door to her and Jill's room was kicked in.

CHAPTER FIFTY-FIVE

Claremorris. Friday, 7:20 pm.
Room service. Was there anything better? Simon accepted the mint-flavoured milkshake while wearing a fluffy hotel dressing gown. He brought the milkshake to his bed, and lay back against the pile of pillows.

Hazel had gone to her own room to get changed but the connecting doors between the two rooms lay open. Simon could see her pulling on a clingy, fluorescent orange dress. He could just imagine Florence's thoughts on seeing it.

Tacky. That was what she would have said.

Before now, Simon might have agreed. But now the loud dress just seemed like an extension of Hazel's personality. Bold. Vibrant. Unapologetic.

He watched her energetic little body move. Hazel didn't have Florence's long legs, but she had a certain earthy charm that made Simon forget about that.

He had a fresh shirt and designer jeans in his bag, but he really didn't feel like attending the party anymore. He took a sip of milkshake. It felt fabulously cold, and the mint flavour was intense. Clearly the chef had blended real mint leaves with high-quality vanilla ice cream, which was an unexpected treat.

He took another sip.

Too much.

"Ugh," he groaned.

"Brain freeze?" Hazel laughed. She appeared in the doorway. "You shouldn't drink it so fast."

The feeling eased a little after a moment. Simon watched Hazel put on a pair of huge hoop earrings.

He said, "Why don't you come back to bed?"

She shook her head. "You better get dressed."

"Do I have to?"

Irritation passed across Hazel's face. The micro-expression was gone quickly, but Simon was sure of what he'd seen. It was so out of keeping with the good time they had just enjoyed together, that he was stunned for a moment.

"Let's go, let's go, let's go," Hazel said.

"Okay," Simon said.

He thought of Florence. Where was she now?

CHAPTER FIFTY-SIX

Claremorris. Friday, 7:21 pm.
Thomas kicked down the door. It only took a second to establish that the room was empty. But someone had been here. A bag lay on one bed, together with the phone he had been tracking. He looked around but saw nothing of value.

His phone rang.

Wendy? The police? It was all the same now. He wanted to turn the phone off, to make sure they couldn't track him, but he still needed it.

So he had to be fast.

He checked the position of the other tracker and found that it was down the hall.

CHAPTER FIFTY-SEVEN

Claremorris. Friday, 7:25 pm.
Florence held her breath as the man – she was sure it was a man – moved around the room next door. She focused on the faint sound of his footsteps. Soon the door closed again. Florence guessed he had found nothing and gone out.

Jill sat on the bed next to Kim, who lay on her side, her hands bound with electrical wire and a pillow case stuffed in her mouth. Not a very dignified position, but Florence stifled her guilt.

Jill said, "Was that—"

"Shush," Florence hissed.

She listened a little longer, wanting to make sure the intruder was really gone. When she heard nothing more, she went and pulled the gag out of Kim's mouth. The pillowcase was wet with saliva.

"Get me up," Kim groaned. "Get me up."

Florence helped her to sit up, with her back resting against the padded head of the bed. But she didn't untie her.

"The gag goes back in if you make a noise," Florence said. "Understand?"

Kim scowled at her, said nothing.

"Who are you?" Florence said.

"An assault victim."

Jill said, "She's got a point, Florence. Things have got out of hand."

"She's not some sweet granny. Not with an encrypted phone and a BS story about being Ronan's aunt. She's been lying to us all day."

Jill still looked uncertain. "Who burst into our room?"

"Good question," Florence said. "Was that a friend of yours?"

Kim scowled even deeper. "You have no idea what you're doing."

"Check her bag," Florence said.

Jill nodded and went to the dressing table. She got the bag and began looking through it.

"Oh my god… Florence, look at this."

"What?"

Jill held up a pistol. "Do you think it's real?"

"It's real alright," Florence said.

Though she did her best to sound calm, her head was spinning. Seeing the gun brought home the reality of what she had done. She'd set all this in motion with a few clicks of her mouse button.

She turned her attention back to Kim.

"Why were you tracking me?"

"Compenso," Kim whispered.

A chill ran down Florence's spine. Despite appearances, Kim really was a gun for hire.

Florence said, "Which one are you? The first or the second."

"The second."

"Oh god."

"So you better let me go before my friend completes the job."

Florence caught sight of Jill's stunned face.

"What's she talking about? Did *you* hire someone to kill Simon?"

"I don't have time to explain it all now. It… it was an accident."

"Some accident."

Jill slipped the gun back into Kim's bag and stepped away, as if she wanted nothing more to do with this situation.

Florence said, "I was drunk. I was heartbroken – he dumped me. I tried to cancel it, but they wouldn't let me. I had to hire a second killer to take care of the first one. I had to make sure he didn't get to Simon."

Jill put her hands on the sides of her head, perhaps to stop it exploding. "This is too much. That's who was next door? A hitman?"

Florence nodded.

"And the second assassin is… this granny?"

Kim cleared her throat. "Young lady, I can assure you, I have no grandchildren. And I'm not as old as I look. Now let me go."

"Should we tell Deb?" Jill said.

"No way. I'd go to jail for a hundred years. And don't forget, you helped me. You'd be in trouble too."

Unease still clouded Jill's face.

"We can get out of this," Florence said.

"How?"

"I'm working on it. I need you to find out more about who that man is."

"I saw a photo of some guy on her phone. Maybe that's him."

Florence picked up Kim's phone. She found the picture Jill mentioned. It was easy to find as it was the only photo in the phone's gallery. It made sense that she had a photo of her target.

"Is this him?" Florence read his name. "Thomas Ogden?"

"It doesn't matter," Kim said. "Your only hope is to let me go."

"I don't think so."

Florence wasn't ready to trust her. She went to the table and picked the gun out of Kim's bag, surprised at how heavy it was. The cold steel made her skin prickle. She slipped it back inside the bag, so she wouldn't have to touch the weapon directly, then swung the bag over her shoulder

"Find out more about these people," Florence said. "Compenso is the name they use."

"Compenso," Jill repeated. "Okay. Where are you going?"

"I need to talk to Simon."

CHAPTER FIFTY-EIGHT

London. Friday, 7:32 pm.
The fundraiser was being held at a townhouse in Notting Hill. Two security guards stood at the bottom of the steps. They looked at each other when they saw Archie, but they said nothing.

He and Lucinda passed up the steps and through the open door. They were greeted in the hall by two waiters with Champagne flutes. The waiters wore tuxedoes too.

"Glad I'm not the only penguin," Archie whispered.

Lucinda slapped his arm playfully. "It's black tie, Archie. Everyone has a tux."

They followed a red carpet down the hall into a huge ballroom. More waiters were circulating with canapes.

Archie recognised many familiar faces, including the host, a former Member of Parliament, who had asked Archie not to come. Like that was going to happen. This whole thing was his idea. He wasn't going to miss the event just because he'd lost his job.

At the top of the room, a jazz band was setting up. The guitarist struck his first chord. Mellow and easy, the sound resonated through the room.

"Shall we jump right in and dance?" Lucinda said.

"I—" Archie's phone buzzed. He reached into his pocket and checked it, making Lucinda roll her eyes.

"Can you leave that thing alone?"

"Yeah," Archie said, without looking. He was too intent on the message he'd received. It was from his source in the Metropolitan Police.

Your man has been compromised. He left his wallet near Brompton Cemetery with the victim's. They're already at his house.

"Oh, god."

Lucinda's unhappy expression deepened.

"What is it, Archie? Is it the children?"

Their kids were now in their forties, but Lucinda still worried about them as if they were new-borns.

"No, it's not the children. I have to make a call."

"Can't it wait?" Lucinda said. "What's so important?"

Archie didn't answer. Instead, he hurried outside.

CHAPTER FIFTY-NINE

Claremorris. Friday, 7:35 pm.
When Florence left the room, Jill began frantically browsing darknet forums. There was a lot of hacker know-how in these places. People boasting about the latest exploits. Selling packages of code.

That foreign word Florence had mentioned, *compenso*, sounded familiar. Jill was sure she'd heard it before, but she couldn't remember where or why. She had asked Kim about it, but the older woman remained silent.

Kim's mouth hung open and her breathing was laboured. She was obviously in pain, her wrists bound tightly behind her back. Jill hated to see her like that. Kim reminded her of her grandmother.

It was hard to believe that *this* was what an assassin looked like. Kim looked just like anyone, certainly more harmless than most. Jill would have thought Florence was deluded, if they hadn't found the gun.

"How are you feeling?" Jill said.

"You need to let me go."

"I can't." Jill scrolled quickly through another forum. Nothing. The darknet had search engines, just like the Clearnet – the publicly accessible internet that most people used. Jill tried another search engine now, looking for *compenso* and *killers*.

Then she found it. The explanation she'd been looking for.

"Oh my god."

Florence needed to be told what she'd learnt as soon as possible.

Jill looked at Kim. The older woman's eyes were closed and her breath had become even louder. Jill hurried to her side. What was happening? Had she stopped breathing?

"Are you alright?"

She reached behind Kim's back, where her hands were bound, and loosened the electrical wire to provide the older woman with some relief.

How did CPR work? Did you start by pounding their chest or by breathing into the person's mouth? Why had she never taken a first aid course?

"Kim—"

Bam.

Kim's forehead came down on the bridge of Jill's nose.

There was pain. And blood.

An explosion of red.

Jill fell on the floor, stunned. She watched helplessly as Kim waddled past her, moving unsteadily towards the door. She dropped the electrical wire on the floor as she went.

CHAPTER SIXTY

Claremorris. Friday, 7:36 pm.
Florence hurried down the corridor and around the corner. Looking at the GPS map on Kim's phone, she could see the dot representing herself.

A second dot was also moving quickly. She figured that might be the man who had kicked down the door to her room. Kim was supposed to stop him. Yet Florence couldn't see that Kim had much of an effort. She'd been content to get a lift with Florence and sleep most of the journey.

What kind of sense did that make? Florence couldn't understand it.

The third dot on the map was stationary. That had to be Simon. Florence headed for that dot.

She found herself standing in front of a room in the middle of a long corridor. She knocked and waited.

Was Simon still okay? What if she was too late? What if the killer had already done the job?

She knocked again. Harder.

The door swung open, revealing Simon's face.

Florence beamed.

"Oh, thank god. You're alive."

Simon's man-bun was untied, his black hair hanging loose behind his ears. He wore a crisp shirt. Only a few of the buttons were closed. He was wearing jeans, but his feet were bare. He must have been preparing to go down to the party.

Irritation passed over Simon's face. Then something else. Tenderness? Guilt? But what did he have to feel guilty about?

"Of course, I'm alive," Simon said. "What are you doing here?"

Florence felt like crying. The relief was that strong.

"I've done something terrible, Simon, but I'm going to straighten things out."

"What are you talking about?"

"It's a long story."

And it would sound insane if I tried to tell you.

Movement in the corner of Florence's eye startled her. She looked back the way she had come.

Kim stood at the end of the hall.

There was a spatter of blood on her cheek, and her eyes were dark.

How the hell did she get free? Where was Jill?

Kim began walking slowly towards Florence. She looked angry.

"Fiat justitia…" Kim said.

Florence squinted at her. "What?"

A male voice boomed, "… ruat caelum."

Florence dropped the phone in surprise. She spun around. The guy whose image she had seen on Kim's phone stood at the other end of that corridor. Thomas Ogden. The first hitman. The one she had hired to kill Simon.

He too began walking towards Florence.

Simon stepped forward and poked his head out of the room to see what was happening. He had no idea how much danger he was in.

Florence gave him a push. "Get back inside, Simon."

"What the hell is going on? Are they with you?"

"Inside. Get inside."

He stepped back, a confused expression on his face.

Florence turned her attention to Kim.

"I paid you to do a job. So do it. Be a professional. Do your thing."

Kim kept coming, slowly.

"You have no idea what my thing is," Kim said. "People like you? You're scum."

"People like me?" Just then, Florence's phone rang. It was Jill. Not the best time for a chat, but Florence answered. "They're here," Florence said. "Both of them."

Jill said, "They're not who you think they are."

The man was halfway down the hall. So was Kim, on the other side. They were blocking Florence in. There was nowhere to go.

"Make it quick, Jill. I can only speak for a few seconds."

"Okay. I found out what Compenso is. I knew I'd heard it before, and I found a forum—"

"Give me the fucking executive summary."

"They're not assassins."

"Of course they are."

"No. They're *vigilantes*."

Kim had almost reached her. So had Thomas. A hammer hung from his hand.

"I don't understand," Florence said.

Jill spoke rapidly. "I'd heard about them. I remembered it when I saw what people were saying about them on the darknet. They're extremist vigilantes. They entice people into hiring them to kill someone."

"And then?"

"They kill the person who hired them, not the supposed target. They want to rid the world of evil. They're not assassins. They're taking out the trash."

And I'm the trash, Florence thought.

"Florence, they're not after Simon. They're after you."

CHAPTER SIXTY-ONE

Claremorris. Friday, 7:39 pm.
The altercation with Jill had taken a lot out of Kim.
She hadn't thought she'd have to brawl with
someone. It wasn't a great idea, not in her state of
health. The headbutt had probably hurt Kim more
than Jill. Even as she bore down on Florence, Kim
felt dizzy and weak, and a pain shot down her left
arm.

No, she thought. *Not now.*

She'd come here to do a job.

True, killing Thomas Ogden had *not* been that job.
Imperator had simply asked her to observe Thomas
because he was worried about him. Worried that he
was starting to enjoy the work for its own sake. It
seemed that Thomas had lost sight of the big picture,
of the reason Compenso existed: to ensure justice
was done, to punish those who sought to harm others.

As a matter of personal interest, Kim had also
wanted to see the kind of person who hires two

different killers within twelve hours. She wanted to watch Florence Lynch die.

But Kim's health, or her lack of health, was catching up on her a little too soon. And she hated that.

She forced herself to move down the corridor. As Florence ducked into Simon Hill's hotel room, Thomas Ogden strode purposefully on.

Let justice be done...

Kim had felt it necessary to reveal herself to Thomas as a fellow operative, because his help might be necessary. She didn't want to end up fading away in a hospital far from home. Kim wanted to go out in a bang.

CHAPTER SIXTY-TWO

Claremorris. Friday, 7:41 pm.

The door slammed shut. Thomas Ogden ignored it for the moment. He was more interested in the woman. Archie had told Thomas nothing about a second operative working on the case.

The woman fell to her knees, clutching her chest.

Thomas walked over and looked down on her. "Why are you here?"

"To watch."

"The truth, please?"

The woman's mouth opened and closed. She looked like a fish gasping for oxygen.

"Florence Lynch placed a second order when we wouldn't cancel the first job. She ordered a hit on you."

Thomas shook his head, a roguish grin of disbelief spreading across his face.

"You took the job? And you came her to kill me?"

"No." The woman's voice trembled. "We took the money, but I'm not here to kill you."

Thomas said, "I don't believe you."

He let the hammer swing like a pendulum between his finger and thumb.

The woman spoke with an effort. "Imperator... asked... me to..."

She collapsed on her side. One eye was shut, one still open. She seemed to be having a heart attack. Thomas hoped she'd finish her explanation before she died. He hunkered down and shook her shoulder.

"Imperator asked you to what?"

"To watch you... He said you're... too eager..."

The woman gasped, her breath coming quick and shallow.

A ringtone sounded nearby. Thomas got to his feet and spun around. A phone was lying on the carpet. Florence had dropped it before she went inside the room.

"That's... mine..." the woman gasped.

Thomas picked it up, noting that it was an encrypted phone, though it was currently unlocked. Florence seemed to have got past the biometrics. Surprising. He hit the green button.

A distorted voice spoke. "Fiat justitia..."

Archie.

Thomas said, "... ruat caelum."

He figured that his own voice would be distorted to the caller. Archie would not be able to tell who had answered the call. Not even if it was a woman or a man. He'd think he was speaking to the woman crumpled on the carpet.

Archie said, "I've received some information from a source in the Metropolitan Police. They've ID'd Thomas Ogden." Thomas already knew that his wallet had been found. But he was impressed that the news had got to Archie so quickly. "The plan has changed. Mr. Ogden cannot be allowed to return to London."

I won't, Thomas thought.

Out loud, Thomas said, "You want him dead?"

"Unfortunately, it's necessary for the cause," Archie said. "We have no idea what he'd say. We must do it for the good of others."

"Of course."

"Are you willing to do what must be done?"

Thomas smiled. "I am."

"Thank you."

Thomas ended the call and pocketed the phone.

He guessed that was why the woman had really been sent here. Archie had wanted her to kill Thomas, even if he hadn't told her that earlier. Thomas being exposed had just made it more urgent.

Thomas took out his own phone and brought up the draft e-mail he had prepared. The one which revealed Archie Browne to be the shadowy Imperator, the mastermind behind Compenso. He hit *send* and the e-mail went to the Metropolitan Police, Cyber Crime Unit, plus five of London's biggest media organisations, to make sure Archie's friend in the police was unable to bury this.

So sad that things had gone astray. It was disruptive to Thomas's work. And sad too that no one would appreciate the work he'd done.

Brook Reynolds's wife probably thought Thomas was an evil thug. She had no idea that she owed her life to Thomas. After all, it was her husband who had hired Thomas to kill her, just so he could be with his mistress and avoid a messy divorce. Now *that* was evil. All Thomas had done was eliminate some scumbags. Now he had to run to preserve his liberty.

Fleeing his old life was disruptive, but he would adapt. And he'd continue his work somewhere else, under some other name.

And damn if it wasn't becoming more fun with every kill.

Thomas hunkered down next to the woman and checked her pulse.

She was dead.

CHAPTER SIXTY-THREE

Claremorris. Friday, 7:43 pm.
Florence had pushed Simon into the room, then slammed the door shut and pressed her back against it. She recalled the sound of Thomas Ogden kicking down the door of her own room. He was strong. Of course he was. He was a killer.

Actually, a *vigilante*.

She was still trying to digest what Jill had found out. That Thomas Ogden did indeed kill people, just not the ones he was hired to kill.

She slumped to the floor, her back still pressed to the door, in case he tried to enter the room.

Simon stared at her like she was crazy. She'd thought she was coming here to protect him, but now she was the one who needed help.

Simon said, "If this is some attention-grabbing ploy—"

"That man in the corridor wants to kill me."

Simon laughed. "He can join the club."

"I mean literally. He wants to murder…"

Her voice broke on the word *murder.*

"What are you talking about? You're… you're serious?"

She nodded. "I am."

Simon played with the buttons of his shirt, as if uncertain what to do.

"Florence… why? How? I mean… should I call Deb? We were just about to go down."

Florence didn't answer. Instead she thought frantically. What she needed was a way out.

She heard talking from the corridor. Why hadn't he come for her yet? What was he doing out there? And Kim – what was she up to?

Florence hoped Jill was okay. Her PA had thrown herself into this mess without knowing a thing about it. For a second, Florence hated herself for her selfishness. And for not even realising she was being selfish.

She noticed a drink on the nightstand next to Simon's bed.

"Is that a milkshake?"

She thought back to her fridge at home. She had a tub of organic artisan ice cream in the freezer section. Mint flavour. It was what Simon yearned for after they'd spent a night in bed together.

Before Simon could reply, there was movement in Florence's peripheral vision. She realised that the door to the adjoining room was open.

Thomas Ogden?

No, Hazel.

She wore a hideous orange dress and eight-centimetre heels.

"Hello Florence."

Hazel walked across the room to Simon, the sound of her heels echoing off the walls. She put her arms around him and kissed his cheek.

A pain worse than any she had yet felt swelled up within Florence.

"Hazel? What is this?"

Tears clouded her vision but she could still see the smug look on Hazel's face. It was the same expression Florence had seen back in their schooldays, when Hazel stole her first boyfriend, Colm Quinn. The pain of that betrayal still stung. Colm had been so cute in his basketball uniform. Florence had only been going out with him for a fortnight when Hazel seduced him. Florence tried to fight back, throwing herself at him, but Colm wasn't interested in her anymore. In the aftermath, Hazel had the gall to act like she was the injured party. Florence hated her for a while and she didn't date anyone else until her college years.

She forgave Hazel eventually and thought all that was behind them. Thought they had really become friends in the years since school.

Florence wondered if Hazel had set Simon up with Florence just so she could steal him away. That would require true evil.

Suddenly Thomas Ogden kicked the door. Florence cried out and a wave of pain jolted down her spine. Florence reached blindly into Kim's handbag, trying to find the gun.

Another kick on the door. Florence screamed. She could hear the wood splintering. Gripping something metal, she jerked her hand out of the bag.

She looked at what was on the end of her finger.

A ring.

There was no diamond on this one, though.

It was the pin from a grenade in Kim's handbag.

CHAPTER SIXTY-FOUR

Claremorris. Friday, 7:49 pm.
Things happened fast, and to Florence it was a blur. Once she realised she'd pulled the hand grenade's pin, she was terrified. She wondered how long she'd have until it exploded. Seconds?

The door behind her shook in its frame, sending a fresh burst of pain darting through her back. She cried out and pushed Kim's handbag, with the grenade in it, away from her, as hard as she could. It slid across the polished floor, coming to a stop at Simon and Hazel's feet.

Florence counted.

One second.

Another bang on the door. The wood splintered above her head. Florence rolled to the side as Thomas Ogden kicked the door down.

Two seconds.

He burst into the room, a claw hammer raised and ready to swing. His eyes roved the room, looking for

Florence. He paused when he saw Simon and Hazel. Hazel wasn't smiling anymore. Still, she looked more surprised than scared.

Three seconds.

Florence rolled again, her heart in her chest, towards the doorway of the adjoining room. She couldn't catch her breath. She had to get away.

Four seconds.

She threw herself into the next room as the grenade detonated.

The sound was tremendous. Its blast shook the room.

Plaster from the wall rained down and smoke filled the air. Florence cradled her head to block out the sound of a woman screaming.

That sound didn't last long.

Silence fell.

Thick, heavy silence.

Trembling all over, Florence got to her feet. She didn't want to look, but she knew she had to. She walked back into Simon's room.

Simon and Hazel were both down on the floor. They were covered in blood and dirt. Simon's glassy eyes stared at the ceiling. Hazel's were closed.

They were both dead.

How was this possible? Everything had gone so wrong in twenty-four hours.

A groan made Florence turn. It was him. The killer.

Of course Thomas Ogden *would* survive. How did it always work out like that? The worst of people seemed to make it out of bad situations.

He was lying on the floor. His T-shirt was torn at the belly and blood was soaking into the fabric. His neck was cut too. He opened his mouth to speak but all that came out was a spatter of blood.

Florence wanted to shoot him, but Kim's handgun had been in the bag with the grenade. It must have been damaged. But Thomas's hammer lay on the floor and that looked alright.

Thomas Ogden had taken her money, betrayed her, and planned to kill her with this brutal tool. She didn't feel like he deserved any mercy.

Voices came from the corridor. People were coming to see what had happened.

Florence had to be fast. She took off her scarf and wrapped it around the hammer so her fingerprints wouldn't be on it.

Thomas's eyes widened.

He tried to speak again.

"Tell Wendy that—"

Florence didn't want to hear anything he had to say. She bent her back, gripped the hammer with both hands, and swung, smashing it into the side of Thomas's head as hard as she could.

Once.

Twice.

He was dead on the third swing, the side of his head a gory mess of blood and cracked skull.

She walked over to Hazel and carefully touched the hammer's handle against Hazel's hand to get some fingerprints on it, then dropped it next to her best friend's body.

A moment later, Jill appeared in the open doorway. Her nose was bloody but otherwise she looked alright.

She said, "Oh my god, what happened?"

Florence ignored the question. She was focusing only on what she needed to do. Her survival instinct had taken over.

"Where's my laptop?"

Jill seemed dazed. Florence shook her by the shoulders.

"The laptop?"

"In our room," Jill said slowly. Her voice was tiny. She stared at the bodies.

Florence dragged her out onto the corridor. People were coming running, drawn by the sound of the explosion.

"Come on, Jill," Florence said. "You need a brandy or something. And I do too."

CHAPTER SIXTY-FIVE

London. Friday, 7:55 pm.
Lucinda's face hadn't lost its shadow of suspicion ever since Archie disappeared into the night to make that mysterious phone call. When he returned to the fundraiser, he'd done his best to placate her. It was nothing, he said. Just a call.

"What about?" Lucinda asked.

Archie tried to shake it off, said it was nothing important. But his face gave him away.

Twenty minutes later, they were dancing a waltz and Lucinda was still giving him dirty looks.

Then there were voices behind him. The band kept playing, but some guests stopped dancing.

"Archie. What do those men want?"

He followed his wife's gaze. Two young police officers stood behind him. Two more stood by the door. He could see the flash of red and blue lights in the hallway from a police car on the street. He could tell at once that they were about to take him into custody.

"What's going on?" Lucinda asked.

Archie took a long, slow breath.

It's okay, he thought.

"I'll be back soon," Archie said. "It appears that these officers need my assistance."

He gave Lucinda a kiss.

That was when the band fell silent. The nearest officer opened his mouth to speak.

"Not here," Archie said. "Outside please. Then you can say whatever you want to say to me."

The officer hesitated for a moment, then nodded.

"Archie?"

He felt Lucinda's hand on his arm.

"Don't worry about me," he said.

Gently he pulled away from her. He gazed at her for a moment, burning her image into his mind. Then he turned and walked towards the door, two police officers walking ahead of him and two following close behind.

He could see the stunned faces of the guests. And the sour face of the host.

He waited until he was in the hall before he pulled the cyanide pill from his jacket pocket and swallowed it.

Let justice be done though the heavens may fall.

The police officers began shouting.

"Hey!"

"Watch out!"

"He took something."

But it was too late. Archie was already gone.

CHAPTER SIXTY-SIX

Claremorris, Friday, 8:01 pm.
Florence dragged Jill down the corridor. Hotel staff were running in the other direction while guests stood outside their doors, drawn by the sound of the blast.

They reached their room and Florence pushed Jill inside. Of course, there was no brandy there. But she went to the fridge and got a half bottle of Chardonnay. She found a glass and filled it, then thrust it into Jill's hand.

"You've had a nasty shock. Drink this. You'll feel better."

Jill looked at the wine as if she didn't know what it was.

What was Florence going to do? She needed to clean things up.

"Drink it down," Florence said.

Jill did.

Florence said, "We don't want anyone to think we're involved in that mess. We should probably delete everything on the laptop. Just to be safe. Can you do that?"

No response. Oh, fuck, Jill was in shock.

"Jill, talk to me. Can you do that? Wipe my laptop clean?"

"Yeah." Jill blinked quickly and looked at Florence, as if she were emerging from a daze. "I can."

"Good. We don't want any misunderstanding."

Florence guided her to the laptop.

There were frantic shouts from the hall.

Suddenly Florence felt sad. She wanted to hear a reassuring voice. Someone telling her everything would be alright.

Daddy.

She took out her phone and called him. There was no answer. She rang again, pacing while she listened. Still there was no answer.

"I've done it," Jill said.

"Good. It's to protect us both."

Jill still seemed dazed.

Florence walked up behind her. She had the sudden urge to strangle the life out of Jill. She could use her hands. Or the electrical wire in Kim's room. It would all be over very quickly.

It would almost be painless.

What am I doing? Florence thought. *I'm not a killer.*

She took off her scarf and put it around Jill's neck in a vain effort to warm her up. Then she walked around Jill, so they were facing each other.

245

"I'm sorry for dragging you into this, Jill. I really am."

Florence walked to the door.

Jill looked up. She said, "Where are you going?"

Florence swallowed. "I'm going to do the right thing."

She stepped out into the corridor. As she walked towards the elevator, she tried calling her father again. Still no answer. This time, she left a voicemail.

"I wish you'd pick up, Daddy. I need you. I love you."

She ended the call and took the elevator to the lobby. She made her way around the reception desk, where a group of staff members were gathered together, whispering to each other. A sign pointed to the function room where Ronan's party was being held.

Would anyone still be there?

She pushed open the door. Music hit her, and colourful lights. There must have been two hundred people in the room, some seated at tables, some standing at the bar to the side of the room, and others dancing on the floor in front of the DJ. Clearly they knew nothing about the carnage upstairs.

Ronan was standing by a table chatting to someone. He looked like he was having a great time. When he saw Florence, he danced his way over. As he got closer, the smile dropped off his face.

"Are you okay? You look kind of… Where's Simon and Hazel?"

"Where's Deb?" Florence said.

Ronan turned and caught his wife's eye. He beckoned her over. Deb came over and exchanged a glance with her husband. Unlike him, Deb seemed alert and sober.

"What's wrong, Florence?" she said.

"He's dead."

"Who is?"

Florence wiped tears from her eyes.

She thought of her father that morning. The disappointment in his eyes that she had failed to behave well.

You know, I think I was too soft on you when you were growing up. I shouldn't blame you. It isn't your fault you're spoilt.

Better Confess. That was where all this started. Florence knew what she had to do.

"I want to report a crime. Can you take me to the station?"

"Do you want to tell me about it?"

Florence shook her head.

"Okay," Deb said in a gentle voice. "Let's go there together."

She guided Florence out of the room and across the lobby. More people had gathered around the reception desk now. Deb took in the scene, but kept moving, walking Florence out the door, and across the car park to her car. An ambulance pulled in at the front of the hotel.

Florence could tell that Deb wanted to speak to the medics and see what was happening. Florence didn't want to wait. She urgently needed to unburden herself, to finally do the responsible thing.

"Can we go?" Florence said.

"Sure."

They went.

CHAPTER SIXTY-SEVEN

Claremorris, Friday, 8:17 pm.

Claremorris Garda Station was a boxy, modern building in the middle of the town. Deb parked around the corner and she and Florence walked inside together.

The uniformed officer behind the desk had a wide, friendly face. He winked at Deb and said, "Nice dress, detective."

Deb ignored him. She guided Florence to a door, where she keyed a code into the panel on the wall. It unlocked with a beep.

"Come on," Deb said gently.

Florence let herself be led down a corridor, past a couple of uniforms and a plainclothes officer, until Deb stopped at a desk with a photo of Ronan sitting on it.

The station had a friendly atmosphere. Florence could hear the murmur of conversation from the other officers. It sounded so good-natured. So wholesome. So completely at odds with what had happened a short distance away.

Deb nodded to a swivel chair. "Sit down, Florence. Do you want a cup of tea?"

"No," Florence said. She eased herself into a creaking chair. Suddenly she felt cold. Cold and sad. Simon was gone forever.

Deb took a seat on the other side of her desk. She moved her computer monitor to the side so they could see one another.

"Are you ready to talk to me?"

"I can't talk about this. But I'd like to make a statement. Can I write it down? Maybe on your computer?"

Deb nodded. "You'd be saving us time. We spend half the day transcribing handwritten statements."

Deb turned on the computer. After a few mouse clicks, she got up from the chair.

"It's all yours."

Florence took her seat. She looked at the computer. A blank document filled the screen.

"I'll go and make us that tea," Deb said. "You can start writing."

She gave Florence's shoulder a squeeze, then left her alone.

For a while, Florence stared at the monitor. Slowly, she began typing.

I did something terrible. Simon said he didn't want to be with me and I was so crazy with jealousy that I hired someone to kill him. Simon Hill is dead because of me.

Her eyes flooded with tears. She let them stream silently down her face. After a moment, she pulled herself together. She found a tissue in her coat pocket. Her bottle of Chanel was there too. She blew her nose, then gave herself a fortifying squirt of perfume.

What had happened was awful.

That was true.

But was it really Florence's fault? Simon had to accept some share of the blame. He knew she had a bad temper. He should have anticipated a strong reaction when he dumped her. A violent reaction even.

And Hazel. She had been trying to ruin Florence's life for years. She'd posed as a friend, but she was only waiting to stab Florence in the back. She was no great loss to the world.

Deb appeared with a cup of tea in each hand.

"Here you go, Florence. How are you getting on? We're hearing that there was an incident at the hotel involving Simon and Hazel. Is that what this is about?"

Florence stared at the cup of tea for a long moment.

Something inside her twisted. A wave of defiance. The surge of her survival instinct moving up a gear.

She sat up straighter in the chair.

"I don't want tea, Deb. I don't drink it. Please bring me coffee and some biscuits. A decent coffee and lots of biscuits."

Deb looked taken aback, but she said, "Okay."

Florence dug a business card out of her wallet. It was printed on thick card, and the name of her solicitor was embossed on the card in gold lettering. She handed it to Deb and said, "Please direct my solicitor to come here immediately. And have him contact my father."

Deb gave her a look, then disappeared down the corridor.

Florence turned her attention back to the computer. She had a fresh idea. Most of what she had already written was fine. She just changed a few words.

Jill did something terrible. Simon said he didn't want to be with her and Jill was so crazy with jealousy that she hired someone to kill him. Simon Hill is dead because of Jill.

Florence sat back and smiled.

That was much better.

No one could contradict her except Jill. And Jill was a loser, a tattooed anarchist hacker who grew up in a pig-pen and walked around with a chip on her shoulder. Florence's legal team would tear her to shreds. And in the unlikely event that they couldn't, there was always another option.

Florence wasn't sure if Compenso still existed, but there must be other people like them. And they'd be happy to take care of Jill for a reasonable price.

Maybe on Jill's doorstep. Two bullets in the back of the head. That was the professional way, Florence had heard, and Florence appreciated professionalism.

Printed in Great Britain
by Amazon

17857731R00148